DOCTOR WHO AND THE NIGHTMARE OF EDEN

DOCTOR WHO AND THE NIGHTMARE OF EDEN

Based on the BBC television serial by Bob Baker by arrangement with the British Broadcasting Corporation

TERRANCE DICKS

A TARGET BOOK
published by
the paperback division of
W. H. ALLEN & Co. Ltd

A Target Book
Published in 1980
by the Paperback Division of W.H. Allen & Co. Ltd
A Howard & Wyndham Company
44 Hill Street W1X 8LB

Reprinted 1982

Novelisation copyright   Terrance Dicks 1980
Original script copyright © Bob Baker 1979
'Doctor Who' series copyright © British Broadcasting
Corporation 1979, 1980

Printed in Great Britain by
Hunt Barnard Printing Ltd, Aylesbury, Bucks.

ISBN 0 426 20130 2

Contents

1

Warp Smash

It should have been impossible – but it happened.

So enormous are the distances between the stars that even at light-speed, journeys of hundreds, even thousands, of years are necessary to cross them. Only the invention of warp drive made interstellar travel a practical possibility. Warp drive enables space ships to leave normal space and enter hyperspace, travelling colossal distances in a flash.

Once man discovered warp drive his space ships spread out over his own galaxy in a wave and even began exploring the galaxies beyond. In time interstellar travel became routine – but there were still dangers. One of them was warp smash.

A ship tries to leave hyperspace at exactly the same point occupied by another; two sets of atoms and molecules try to fill the same position in space and time; the result, instant mutual annihilation. However, there were exceptions, freak accidents in which the impossible happened.

This was to be one of them.

The Intersellar Cruise Liner *Empress* flashed through hyperspace en route for the pleasure-planet Azure, sun-kissed jewel of the galaxy, where her hundreds of tourist passengers could indulge themselves in all the pleasures of warm seas, perpetually blue skies, and long beaches of fine blue sand. Their journey was almost over. Soon the *Empress* would emerge into normal space and enter landing orbit around the planet.

In the big old-fashioned control room of the *Empress*, Captain Rigg was feeling worried, and was trying to work out why. There didn't seem to be anything to worry about. The spacious control room was functioning with its usual calm efficiency. The *Empress* was old now, but she had been solidly built in the vintage years of space travel. Her computerised controls could have flown and landed the ship almost without human aid. Secker, the navigator, certainly wasn't worried. He was lounging at his instrument console, smiling vaguely, completely and utterly relaxed.

That was the trouble, Rigg decided. Secker was *too* relaxed. Re-entry from hyperspace was one of the traditional crisis-points in space travel – just like take-off and landing in the good old days of powered atmospheric flight. Any good spaceman ought to be a little worried at a time like this. There should be a tension, an awareness that, although this might be only the latest of hundreds of uneventful re-entries, it was possible, however unlikely, that something could go wrong.

Perhaps it was just because Secker was so young. Rigg himself was a tough, balding veteran, near the age-limit for a space pilot. He had never flown with Secker before, though he knew that the young man was reputed to be one of the most brilliant navigators in the service. 'We seem to be a little ahead of schedule, Secker.'

'Great! Sooner we get in the better.'

Rigg flicked the intercom switch. 'Captain here. We are coming out of warp drive in thirty seconds. Standard passenger announcement, please.'

In the passenger area, bored and weary tourists were dozing, viewing video cassettes, listening to stereo tapes, nibbling snacks, eating and drinking and chatting with their neighbours. The space coveralls and protective goggles they all wore made them look terrifyingly similar, like rows of dolls on a production line.

There was a musical chime and an inhumanly calm and soothing voice. 'This is your flight computer speaking. We are about to leave warp drive and re-enter normal space in orbit around the planet Azure. Passengers may leave their seats when the blue light comes on, but are requested not to remove their protective coveralls until instructed.' There was a pause as the lights on the display panel flicked from blue to amber, and then to red. 'Passengers are requested to remember that the *Empress* will be at seven-tenths G upon re-entry. Please be careful when you start to move around.'

The warning was a very necessary one. It was not unknown for inexperienced space travellers to leap eagerly from their seats and go hurtling across the cabin.

The passengers settled back, preparing themselves for the odd wrenching sensation that always came on entering and leaving hyperspace.

With a final uneasy glance at Secker, Captain Rigg leaned forward to study the display screen on his console. Like most spacemen, like pilots before them, and like sailors before *them*, Rigg was deeply superstitious. He couldn't help feeling that such careless self-assurance positively invited disaster. He punched up the preset re-entry co-ordinates, and multi-coloured trajectories of light began snaking over the screen. A red light started flashing on Rigg's console. 'I've 'got a malfunction ...' He leaned forward studying the screen. 'Secker, there's a three-degree error in these co-ordinates!'

'What's a few degrees, Skipper?'

'A few degrees?' Rigg was almost choking with rage. 'What's the matter with you, man? We're flying an Interstellar Cruiser, not riding a bike!'

'So?'

'So our orbit will be fractionally out. It'll mean delay in landing.'

Secker shrugged, and Rigg turned angrily away. In actual fact, the error was unlikely to cause much of a problem. It would just mean an extra hour's delay for the impatient tourists. It was the sheer unprofessionalism of Secker's attitude that was so infuriating.

Rigg was about to reset the co-ordinates when there was a fiercely urgent alarm-bleep and red lights flashed all over his console. He looked at the forward-vision screen and gave a gasp of horror.

Another space ship was heading straight towards them.

The other ship was the survey vessel *Hecate*, also en route for Azure. The slender *Hecate* transfixed the huge dematerialising bulk of the *Empress* like an arrow, but astonishingly there was no impact. Instead the *Empress* seemed to materialise around *Hecate*, so that the two ships were locked together in a strange and deadly embrace.

Astonished to find himself still alive, Rigg hit the distress button. 'Emergency! Emergency! Mayday! Mayday! Mayday! Cruise Liner *Empress* reporting space collision on approach to Azure.' He flicked the intercom. 'Bridge here. Damage control report immediately, please.'

Two space-suited crewmen ran down the central corridor of the ship – and stopped in astonishment as they found themselves facing a strange blurred zone, where the two ships seemed to merge. One of them spoke into his hand communicator. 'We've found one of the junction points, sir. It's incredible – as though the two ships were sticking through each other.'

Rigg's voice crackled urgently. 'Any hull leakage? How's the pressure?'

'Everything seems to be normal. But we can't get through to the main passenger section. They're blocked off by the hull of the other ship – it's sticking right through the entrance to B-deck.'

Rigg snapped, 'A-deck, report, A-deck, report. Any casualties?'

There was no reply. He swung round to Secker. 'Any more damage estimates yet?'

Secker smiled foolishly at him. Rigg sprang across the cabin, gripped the younger man by the shoulders and lifted him bodily from his seat. 'This is all your fault, Secker! But it's my responsibility, *I* carry the can. I'll probably lose my job – but I'll see you never work in this galaxy again.' Rigg slid into Secker's place. 'I'll make the damage checks, you check the power. Come on, move yourself. This is an emergency.'

In another part of the ship, close to one of the blurred junction areas, there was a wheezing, groaning sound. A blue police box materialised from nowhere.

A tall curly-haired man in a floppy broad brimmed hat and long trailing scarf came out of the police box and stood looking cautiously about him. He was followed by a small, very pretty fair-haired girl in a neat grey dress. Behind her glided something that looked like a robot dog.

The blue box was in reality a highly sophisticated space/time craft called the TARDIS.

The tall man was that mysterious traveller known as the Doctor, the girl was his companion Romana, and the robot dog was a mobile computer called K9. They had picked up the *Empress*'s Mayday call and the Doctor had been unable to resist the temptation to investigate.

He pointed to the blurred area just ahead of them. 'Just look at that, eh? Isn't that interesting?'

'Fascinating,' said Romana drily. She had never been able to understand the Doctor's habit of rushing straight into trouble at the first available opportunity.

The Doctor moved closer to the blurred area, examining it with interest. It looked like nothing so much as a belt of frozen fog, through which could be discerned the shadowy outlines of the hull of another ship, somehow inside the first. 'Bit of a mishmash, eh?'

'Why wasn't there an explosion?'

'This ship must have been emerging from hyperspace when it all happened. It materialised *around* the smaller one — a sort of a freak accident, very nasty. Now they've really got a problem, haven't they, K9?'

K9 glided forward, scanning the blurred zone with his sensors. 'Affirmative. Matter interfaces at overlapped areas are highly unstable.'

The crash should have caused a shattering explosion that would have destroyed both ships. Now that explosion had been frozen — but if the interfaces gave way, it could take place at any moment. The two linked ships were a highly unstable time-bomb. 'Perhaps we shouldn't interfere?' said Romana hopefully.

The Doctor gave her a puzzled look. 'Not interfere? Of course we should interfere. Always do what you're best at, that's what I say!' He marched off down the corridor.

Resignedly Romana followed. The Doctor had been interfering in another people's problems all his lives. It was too late to expect him to stop now.

They came to the end of the corridor, turned right and found themselves facing a sign that read 'AIR-LOCK'. There was a heavy metal door just beneath the sign – and it was opening.

The Doctor and his companions ducked back round the corner.

A burly, fair-haired man in space coveralls came out of the airlock, glanced round as if to get his bearings, then set off down the main corridor.

'Who's that?' whispered Romana.

'The Captain of the other space ship, I should imagine, coming to make a complaint! Let's follow him, shall we? Should be an interesting encounter.'

They followed the space-suited man through the wide metal corridors until he turned into the doorway of what was obviously the main control room. The Doctor held up his hand and they paused, waiting. After a moment there came the sound of angry voices. The Doctor motioned his companions forward.

They found themselves in a huge, old-fashioned control room, packed with computerised equipment. At the far end was the bridge, a raised control area with seats for pilot and co-pilot, control consoles and viewing screens in front of them. The man they had followed was shouting at a thin, wet, balding man in a black-and-gold uniform, who sat hunched in the pilot's seat. 'What I want to know is, what are you going to do about the damage to my ship?'

The second man punched controls and a computerised chart of the ship appeared on the vision screen. 'All I'm concerned with is the damage to *my* ship and the safety of *my* crew – not to mention several hundred passengers. The *Empress* carries comprehensive insurance, so you needn't worry.'

'I was on my way to a most important survey job when you came crashing in on me. Now you tell me not to worry! What am I going to do for a ship?'

'I'm sure the company will compensate you in full. Why don't you just go back to your ship, wait for the experts to arrive, and get in touch with your insurance people?'

'Don't worry, I will. And I shall insist that you sign a document admitting that the collision was entirely your fault.'

'I'll do no such thing! What were you doing there anyway, right in the middle of a commercial descent-area?'

'I was given full clearance by Azure control. You were the one off course.'

The wrangle went on. The Doctor noticed that there was a third man in the room, a younger man, who watched the argument with a vague foolish smile, as if it didn't really concern him.

The argument between the two Captains raged on, voices getting louder and angrier, charges and counter-charges flying across the room.

The Doctor decided it was time to intervene. He stepped forward. 'Gentlemen, gentlemen, please. Can't we settle this matter amicably?'

The *Empress* Captain glared indignantly at him. 'Who the blazes are you – and what are you doing in my control room. Are you a passenger?'

The Doctor thought hard and came up with a sudden bright idea. 'No, no, I'm with Galactic Salvage. We heard your Mayday call and came to have

14

a look around.' The Doctor went on talking rapidly, before anyone had time to question this rather flimsy story. 'I'm the Doctor and this is my assistant, Romana.' He beamed at the two astonished Captains. 'How do you do?'

Automatically the Captain nodded to Romana. 'How do you do?' His eyes widened as he noticed K9 for the first time. 'What's that?'

The Doctor glanced down. 'That's K9. He's a sort of computer.'

'Looks more like a robot dog. Does it bark?'

'No, but he has been known to bite. Would you be kind enough to introduce yourselves?'

The Captain found himself obeying, without quite knowing why. 'My name's Rigg, I'm the Captain of this vessel.'

'I know that, we've just met! What about these other gentlemen?'

'This is Captain Dymond. He's the Captain of the other vessel involved in this – incident.'

'How do you do?'

Rigg jerked a thumb at the man in the corner. 'That's Secker, my navigator. Now then, Doctor, you say you're in the salvage business? You realise I can't even discuss such matters till I've spoken with Head Office?'

The Doctor said, 'No need to bother them. I've got a much better idea. Why don't we just separate the ships?'

2

The Collector

The two Captains stared at him in astonishment.

'That's impossible,' growled Dymond.

The Doctor beamed. 'I like doing impossible things.'

With her usual air of calm superiority Romana said, 'If it's possible to get into a situation, then it's theoretically possible to get out of it.'

'Now you've spoilt it,' said the Doctor reproachfully.

Romana ignored him. 'At the time of the collision, this ship was partially dematerialised. Therefore, if we can create the same conditions, the ships can be separated again. It's just a matter of exciting the molecules. Put your ship on to full thrust, then throw it into full reverse. It's worked before, you know.'

The Doctor sighed. 'It was more fun when it seemed impossible!'

Thoughtfully Rigg scratched his balding head. 'It might work ...' He went over to the console and began stabbing at controls. 'If I could get any power – which I can't. The collision must have damaged the power circuits.'

The Doctor looked over his shoulder. 'Are you sure you're pressing the right buttons?'

'Well, of course I am!'

The Doctor rubbed his chin. The *Empress* was powered by old-fashioned atomic motors. For safety reasons, her main power unit would be in another part of the ship, operated from the bridge by remote control. 'Can you switch on direct from the power unit?'

'We could – but it's dangerous. We don't really know the full extent of the damage yet.'

Dymond said eagerly, 'It'd be worth a try. Anything's better than being stuck here.' It was clear that Dymond was very anxious to be on his way.

'It could damage your ship,' warned Rigg.

'That's rich – coming from the man who just crashed into me!'

'Now see here, Captain Dymond –'

The Doctor interrupted them both. 'All right, all right! Where's the main power unit? In the stern?'

Rigg nodded. 'Secker will show you. Secker!'

Forgotten until now, the young navigator came forward. Romana noticed that he was pale and sweating, presumably from reaction after the crash.

'Secker, take the Doctor to the power unit,' ordered Rigg.

Secker nodded without speaking and headed for the door. The Doctor followed him, K9 at his heels. Romana made to join them, but the Doctor shook his head. 'It's all right, Romana, we can manage. Why don't you stay here and keep an eye on things.'

Secker had already left the control room and, before Romana could object, the Doctor hurried after him.

Although she didn't show it, Romana was quietly furious at being left behind. Presumably the Doctor was just trying to keep her out of danger – or perhaps he wanted all the credit of being a miracle-worker for himself. There was a broad streak of childish vanity in the Doctor's character, decided Romana.

It soon became clear that she wasn't wanted in the control room either. With forced politeness Captain

Rigg said, 'Well now, Miss – er – Romana, I've got work to do. Why don't you and Captain Dymond go and wait in the VIP lounge? There's a very interesting chap called Professor Tryst in there at the moment, some kind of interplanetary zoologist, I'm sure you'd enjoy talking to him. He's got a fascinating gadget called the CET machine – uses it for collecting specimens. I'm sure he'll be glad to show it to you.'

Romana didn't particularly want to chat to some wandering animal collector, but she nodded resignedly. 'Very well.'

Rigg sprang up and ushered them to the door. 'Just down the main corridor and to the right, you can't miss it.'

Alone in the control room, Rigg went over to the computer console and punched up an information code. After a few moments computerised lettering appeared on the read-out screen. 'GALACTIC SALVAGE: FORMED LONDON EARTH 2068, COMPANY CEASED TRADING 2096'.

Rigg smiled grimly. Just as he'd suspected, this mysterious Doctor wasn't what he pretended to be. The question was, what was he really up to?

Secker led the Doctor and K9 through the long corridors of the *Empress*. There was an air of old-fashioned calm and luxury about the great space cruiser. The broad corridors were softly carpeted, their walls draped in soothing, pastel fabrics. It was hard to realise that the whole ship was in imminent danger of destruction. If the unstable linkage between the two space craft gave way, both ships would be reduced to metallic fragments drifting in space.

Secker halted at a junction, where the main corridor gave way to a narrower, more workmanlike passage. 'You go down there to section five, left into the shuttle bay and then down into level B. You can't miss it.'

The Doctor looked curiously at him. Secker now looked very ill indeed. He was pale and trembling, and the muscle under one eye had developed a nervous twitch. 'I thought your Captain ordered you to *take* me to the power unit?'

'I've told you where it is, haven't I? What's the difference? I've got other things to do. I'm very busy ...'

Abruptly Secker swung round and ran back the way they had come.

The Doctor looked thoughtfully after him. 'There's something odd about that young man's behaviour, K9. I think we'd better see what he's up to.'

'Affirmative, Master.'

Secker was just disappearing down the corridor and the Doctor hurried after him, K9 gliding at his heels.

Secker led them down a side corridor into a plainer, more functional-looking area of the ship. He was hurrying along with a kind of jerky speed, head down, obviously too preoccupied to think that he might be followed. Eventually he disappeared through an open doorway over which was written 'LUGGAGE SECTION'.

Cautiously the Doctor and K9 slipped through the doorway after him. They found themselves in a long, dimly lit room lined with storage racks which held boxes, crates, and bags of every imaginable description. At the far end of the room was a row of lockers, and Secker hurried up to them. Pausing by one of the lockers, he produced an electronic key. There was a faint beep, and the top drawer of the locker slid open. Secker plunged his hand inside, took something out and slumped against the locker as if in sudden relief. Then he slammed the drawer shut and turned away.

Hastily the Doctor and K9 ducked behind a luggage rack. Secker rushed straight past them and disappeared down the corridor.

The Doctor waited a moment and then moved down to the row of lockers. Fishing out his sonic screwdriver, he made a quick adjustment and then held it to the drawer of the end locker. With a faint beep, the drawer slid open, and the Doctor peered inside. At first sight the drawer seemed empty. Then he saw a small plastic phial lying in the corner. He took it out and examined it. The phial was filled with greyish powder, rather like a fine grey ash.

The Doctor unstoppered the phial, sniffed it cautiously and frowned. Kneeling down, he held the phial out to K9. 'See what you can make of this, old chap.'

K9 extruded a sensor aerial, as if sniffing the phial. There was a brief whirring and clicking, then he announced, 'Substance is organic residue, heavily impregnated with a drug commonly known as Vraxoin. This drug is highly addictive and extremely dangerous.'

The Doctor caught his breath in horror. 'Vraxoin!' Hastily he re-stoppered the phial. 'I've seen whole communities, whole planets, destroyed by this stuff. It induces a state of warm complacency, a kind of total, idiotic happiness. When it wears off there are the most agonising withdrawal symptoms. So you take another dose, the cycle repeats itself and soon you're dead!' The Doctor stuffed the phial in his pocket and hurried out of the luggage area.

The VIP lounge was one of the most luxurious parts of the ship, brightly lit, richly decorated, furnished with comfortable chairs and couches, and a machine that dispensed any kind of food or drink you cared to dial for.

In the centre of the room stood a strange, rather ramshackle machine, a complex, many-sided projector with a glowing red crystal crowning its peaked roof. Standing beside the machine was its owner, a lean, tanned, grey-haired man called Tryst. The old-fashioned square-lensed glasses, the fussy manner, and the clipped, slightly Germanic speech all suggested the academic, while the lean body and the deeply tanned skin were those of a man used to outdoor life. In fact you could deduce what Tryst was, just by looking at him, decided Romana. He could only be some kind or archaeologist or zoologist – a scholar who spent most of his life outdoors, on strange and dangerous planets.

A sturdy dark-haired girl in space coveralls was working on the machine. She had been introduced as Della, Tryst's assistant.

Tryst watched her with proprietary pride, holding forth, as he had been doing for some time, on his own life and work.

'It has long been my ambition to be the first inter-planetary zoologist to qualify and quantify every species in our galaxy. One or two more expeditions and I may well achieve it!'

'You've just got back from one expedition and you're already planning another?'

Romana didn't really want to encourage Tryst to go on, but she felt obliged to make at least a show of interest – particularly since Dymond was sitting slumped in a corner, a drink in his hand, not even pretending to listen.

Tryst nodded eagerly. 'The next expedition is always on my mind, my dear young lady – and the next, and the next. Unfortunately it is a question of

21

finance. I was hoping to find a private sponsor on Azure, but this little accident has delayed everything.'

'You're funded privately? I should have thought the Government ...'

'Ah yes, the Government used to fund me, but the galactic recession put a stop to all that. Now all they can do is provide me with free travel facilities on Government-sponsored airlines.' He chuckled wryly. 'First-class facilities, as you see. My machine and I always travel first class.' He patted the projector proudly.

'What exactly is the machine? What does it do?'

'That, my dear young lady, is the Continuous Event Transmitter. The CET machine, for short. An invention of my own. Let me show you!'

Gently moving Della aside, Tryst got behind the machine. The crystal on top glowed bright red as the machine was switched on. Tryst focussed the projector on the opposite wall and suddenly the wall disappeared, to be replaced by an arid, rocky landscape. Twin suns cast a lurid glow over the scene.

Romana smiled. 'It looks as if you've invented the magic lantern!'

Tryst sounded a little hurt. 'What you *see* may appear to be a mere projection. In fact it is the projection of an actual matter transmutation.'

Romana stared at the landscape. It was certainly more than just a flat picture. You could see right into it and she could even see little dust eddies swirling about the rocks. 'You mean that landscape is real?'

Della smiled, pleased by Romana's astonishment. 'In a sense, yes. You see, when we collect specimens for study they are converted into electro-magnetic signals and stored on an event crystal, which can be projected through the machine.'

'There are living creatures in there?'

Tryst nodded proudly. 'Oh yes. And they go on living and evolving in the crystal.' Tryst held up a small crystal cube. 'The image projection enables us to study them whenever we wish, because the flora and fauna are actually existing in the crystal itself. I'm sure you can appreciate what a tremendous technical achievement that is!'

Romana looked disapprovingly at him. 'I wouldn't say that. All you've achieved is a crude form of matter transfer by dimensional control.'

'Crude?' Tryst was appalled.

'The crudest of prototypes. And you could have problems with it.'

'Problems?' spluttered Tryst. 'But it works perfectly.'

'I very much doubt that – particularly under the conditions we're in now. We've just suffered a materialisation collision, remember, a warp smash. It's caused all kinds of unstable matter interfaces. They'll probably affect the dimensional matrix of your machine. Had you thought of that?'

'Young lady, are you claiming that your scientific knowledge is superior to my own?'

Romana did her best to be tactful. 'Well, equal, shall we say?'

Dymond jumped impatiently to his feet. 'I wish you two would stop showing off with your scientific double-talk! When's something going to be done about freeing my ship?'

Romana sighed and turned back to Tryst. 'All I'm saying is, the potential instability of the matter interface ...'

With a groan of protest, Dymond stalked off to the dispenser and dialled himself a large, stiff drink.

Captain Rigg was doing his best to explain things to ground control on the planet Azure, without a great deal of success. 'Yes, I'm aware we've got a serious problem, but we are doing our best to sort it out. Meanwhile we'll stay in quarantine orbit. Yes, I'll keep you fully informed. Captain Rigg out.'

Rigg flicked off the communicator and looked up as the Doctor and K9 hurried in. 'Well, well, the man from the Galactic! How are things in the power room?'

'Never got there. I want to talk to you about that chap Secker.'

'What about him?'

'He wouldn't take me to the power room – he ran away.'

Rigg tried to grapple with this new problem. 'He was behaving oddly even before the crash. Seems to be in a different world.'

'Perhaps he is,' said the Doctor mysteriously. 'Could I have a look at your log?'

'What for?'

'I'd like to see if he's been to any planet where he might have picked up Vraxoin.'

Rigg looked blankly at him. 'This is a simple tourist run, Doctor. Station nine to Azure, Azure to station nine. A straight charter for the whole tourist season.' Like many once-great space ships, the *Empress* had been forced to accept humbler work in her old age.

'What about the passengers, then? One of them could be a carrier.'

'I doubt it, Doctor. They're all thoroughly respectable citizens of Earth on a long-awaited holiday. They've all had pre-vacation security checks, the Azurian authorities insist on it.'

The Doctor frowned. 'Is there anyone else, apart

from the tourist passengers?'

'There's only Tryst. He's a zoologist. We picked him up on station nine. He'd just finished a long expedition. Said he wanted to combine having a holiday with looking for a sponsor.'

'And where had he been on this expedition?'

Rigg shrugged. 'All over the galaxy, as far as I can make out. But he's not carrying any drugs, Doctor. We checked him and his assistant before we let them on board. Any drugs would have shown up then.'

'I'd still like to know where he's been!'

'And I'd still like to know who you are!'

'Me? I told you, I'm with Galactic Salvage.'

'Galactic Salvage went out of business years ago.'

The Doctor looked surprised. 'They did? I wondered why I hadn't been paid recently.'

'That's not good enough, Doctor.'

'That's what I thought,' agreed the Doctor. 'Where do I find this chap Tryst?'

'In the VIP lounge.'

'See if you can find Secker, then meet me there in five minutes.'

Rigg jumped up. 'Look here, Doctor, you still haven't answered –'

'Do you want this ship freed or not?' asked the Doctor severely.

'Well, of course I do.'

'Then meet me in the lounge in five minutes!'

Before Rigg could protest further, the Doctor was gone.

As Secker strolled vaguely along the corridors of the *Empress*, it seemed that he floated cloudlike along a velvet tunnel flecked with gleaming jewels towards some wonderful destination. The only thing to spoil his pleasure was a persistent voice nagging at him. It was calling his name.

'Navigator Secker,' blared the metallic voice. 'Navigator Secker will report to the bridge immediately.'

Secker giggled foolishly and drifted on.

He became aware that the corridor ahead of him ended abruptly in an area that looked strangely like frozen fog. And there was something else, a kind of blue mist that drifted through the grey fog, intermingling with it.

It was all very interesting. Ignoring the still-blaring voice, Secker wandered into the mist.

It swallowed him up.

3

The Attack

'Go on,' said the Doctor, 'Where did you go next?'

Tryst leaned forward eagerly, delighted by the Doctor's flattering interest in his travels.

'We went through the Sigmus Gap and over to System M Three-Seven. It's a small system, only three planets, but one of them supports life in a very early stage of evolution – molluscs, algae, a few primitive insects. Here, I can show you. Della, get me the M Three-Seven crystal.'

Della reached for a rack holding the crystals, but the Doctor held up his hand. 'No, no, please don't trouble yourself. I'm more interested in the voyage itself, the planets you've visited. It's really quite fascinating.'

Tryst took a slim leather-bound volume from a nearby table. 'Here you are, Doctor! *The Log of the 'Volante'*, a full record of all my voyages. I had it published to go with my lectures. The *Volante* was my ship.'

The Doctor flicked through the log, page by page. 'Fascinating, quite fascinating!' He got up and wandered over to the CET machine. 'And you invented this device to collect your specimens? I once knew a scientist who was working on a device like this – a Professor Stein.'

'You knew Professor Stein? He was my closest colleague. We worked on the idea together and I completed the device after his death. Did you know him well?'

'Only by reputation. I once attended his seminar on –'

Dymond said impatiently, 'This scientific reminiscence is all very fascinating, Doctor, but don't we have more important things to do? I thought you were going to help separate the ships. I'm very anxious to be on my way. I hadn't really been expecting a space liner to materialise around my ship today.'

Before the Doctor could reply, Captain Rigg hurried into the lounge. 'I can't locate Secker anywhere, Doctor. I've called him on the intercom all over the ship. Now I've got men out looking for him.'

'I see. Then you'll have to take me down to the power unit yourself, won't you?'

'Very well.'

'Let's be on our way, shall we?' The Doctor turned to Tryst. 'I've enjoyed our chat. We must have a little discussion about that machine of yours sometime – and about the ethics of capturing alien species for your own private zoo.'

Tryst was taken aback. 'Zoo, Doctor? I am engaged in important scientific research, helping to conserve endangered species.'

The Doctor nodded towards the CET machine. 'By putting them in that thing? You're conserving them the way a jam maker conserves raspberries! Come along, Captain.'

As the Doctor left, followed by Rigg and K9, Romana turned to Tryst. 'You mustn't mind the Doctor. He just likes to irritate people.'

'Well, he has a right to his opinion, I suppose,' said Tryst huffily. 'Still, it's nice to have someone of reasonable intellect to talk to again.' He smiled at Della and patted her arm. 'No disrespect, my dear,

28

but after such a long voyage cooped up with the same people ...'

'How many were on your expedition?' asked Romana.

'Just Della and myself. There were three of us to begin with, but we ... lost one. He died.'

Romana saw Della wince.

Tryst seemed to be staring into the past, reliving some horrible event.

'How did he die?' asked Romana.

'He ... died,' repeated Tryst, and turned away.

Rigg took the Doctor and K9 along the service corridors of the *Empress*, towards the power bay. 'Did you learn anything from Professor Tryst, Doctor?'

'No. I checked through all the planets he'd visited. None of them was a known source of Vraxoin. Though mind you ...'

'What?'

'It cropped up on various planets, but it always turned out to have been smuggled in from somewhere else. No one ever discovered where it originated from – or how to make it, come to that.'

'It's a drug, isn't it? Surely it can be copied artificially?'

'Some very eminent scientists tried, when they were looking for a cure for Vraxoin addiction. Vraxoin seems to be a mixture of animal and vegetable elements combined in some unique way. So if someone's found out where it comes from, or how to make it ...'

'He could make a colossal fortune,' said Rigg slowly.

'That's right. And ruin a colossal number of lives in the process – oh dear!'

They turned a corner and found themselves facing

a wall of frozen fog. They had reached a point where the two ships joined. K9 glided forward, extruding his antennae. 'Caution. Area of overlap is highly dangerous. Molecular structure of the two ships is incompatible, causing unstable matter interface.'

The Doctor studied the strange blurred area. 'Fascinating. The ships are rejecting each other – molecularly that is.'

Rigg struggled to understand. 'Like a tissue transplant, you mean?'

'Exactly. At the moment there's a kind of precarious balance, but if it tips one way or the other ... Tell me, is there another way to the power unit?'

'We could try from below the shuttle bay. We'd have to cut through a wall, but it's fairly thin there. I'll get hold of some lasers.'

The Doctor smiled. 'Don't bother – I've got my own equipment!'

He bent down and patted K9.

Left alone in the VIP lounge, Romana wandered over to the CET machine and switched it on. Immediately the wall in front of the machine disappeared, to be replaced by an arid, rocky landscape so real that it looked as if you could walk into it. She flicked the selector switch, and a bare, windy plain replaced the rocks. Next came a forest with a glimpse of a ruined city.

The next projection was of a dense tropical jungle with thick-boled trees, waving palm-fronds, dangling vines and creepers, and a riot of assorted greenery struggling towards the light of a lurid orange sky. The canopy of vegetation was so thick that it was dark and shadowy between the tree trunks. Romana had an uneasy feeling that things were moving in those shadows. Certainly there was life in the jungle –

a weird assortment of squawks, growls and hisses bore witness to that.

There was something curiously hypnotic about the jungle scene. Romana found herself drawn closer and closer to the projection. She had a strange sensation that there was someone in the picture, watching her, a shadowy figure half-hidden behind one of the trees. Romana took a step nearer – and a voice behind her said sharply. 'What are you doing?'

It was Della, Tryst's assistant.

'I was just having a look,' said Romana vaguely. 'I hope you don't mind?'

Della went over to the machine and switched it off. '*I* don't mind, no.'

'Then why switch it off?'

'Because Professor Tryst would mind very much indeed. This machine's his pride and joy. Nobody touches it except him.'

'Has it ever gone wrong?'

'No, why should it?'

Romana studied the machine. 'Lots of reasons. It really is a very primitive device. Could I just see a little more of that last projection?'

'Eden?' said Della sharply. 'No, I'd rather you didn't, if you don't mind.'

'Why not? What's the matter?'

'It's just that Eden brings back very unpleasant memories. That was where we lost Stott, the third member of the crew.'

'Was he a close friend of yours?'

'More than a friend,' said Della quietly. 'Still, it doesn't matter now. If you'll excuse me?' Obviously near to tears, Della rushed from the room.

The Doctor, Rigg and K9 went along more corridors, down in a service lift, along more corridors, only to find themselves facing the frozen fog barrier once again.

Rigg sighed. 'We'll have to try another route, Doctor. The place to cut through is beyond this overlap.'

'Whereabouts is the power unit from here?'

Rigg pointed to the ceiling. 'Up there. We'll have to –'

A blood-curdling scream came from somewhere within the fog.

'Come on,' shouted Rigg and dashed forwards, the Doctor close behind him.

'Caution, Master,' called K9. 'You are entering a matter interface!'

They found themselves in a strange unearthly region, where not only vision but time and motion were blurred as well. It was if they were struggling in some kind of dreamlike slow-motion.

The Doctor stumbled over something soft, moving – a human body. 'Here, Rigg,' he yelled. 'We've got to get him out!'

They bent down, grabbed the body and, with a mighty effort, dragged it out of the interface and back into the corridor.

Gasping Rigg looked down – and saw that they had found the missing Secker. His clothes were ripped and torn as if by savage claws, and blood oozed from deep gashes in his chest and neck.

Rigg snatched out his communicator. 'Emergency medical team to service lift seven, level four. I'll meet you by the lift. Move.' He flicked off the communicator. 'Give me a hand with him, will you, Doctor?'

The Doctor took Secker's shoulders, while Rigg lifted his feet. As they carried the body away the Doctor called, 'Take a look in there K9, see if you can find anything.'

'The mist is a matter interface, and therefore dangerous,' protested K9.

The Doctor sighed. You couldn't expect an automaton to take illogical risks. 'All right, K9, just go to the edge.'

'Affirmative, Master.'

K9 nosed his way cautiously up to the edge of the fog and even ventured a few inches inside. Immediately he felt that same disorientation that had affected the Doctor and Rigg. 'Sensors will not function in this environment, Master. Expedition useless.'

By the time they reached the lift, a medical team was waiting for them. Rigg helped them to lift Secker's body on to the stretcher. 'Get him to sickbay, right away.'

The medics carried the stretcher into the lift, Rigg followed them, and the doors closed.

Left on his own, the Doctor stood thinking hard for a moment. He knew now what had happened to Secker – but what about Secker's supply of Vraxoin. He turned and hurried back the way he had come.

The luggage compartment was still dark and shadowy as the Doctor approached – but this time it wasn't empty. A figure was hunched over Secker's locker. At the sound of the Doctor's footsteps, the figure darted back into the shadows.

The Doctor strode into the room and looked around. He went down the room towards the locker, found the open drawer and peered inside. It was empty.

The Doctor stared down at the drawer, rubbing his chin. He had arrived too late – but at least he knew that Secker had a confederate in his drug smuggling. Someone else on the ship was involved as well – and that someone had lost no time in getting hold of

Secker's supply of Vraxoin. But where was Secker's accomplice now?

A shuffling movement in the shadows made the Doctor realise that the one he was seeking could be right behind him. The Doctor spun round and saw a glimpse of a goggled, space-coveralled figure holding a blaster.

The Doctor backed away, talking frantically to gain time. 'Hullo! Now, please don't do anything hasty. I'm sure we can talk this over –'

The Doctor was planning to hurl himself aside, but he left it too late. The blaster fired, catching him full in its energy-beam. The Doctor writhed, staggered, then pitched headlong to the floor. Stooping over the Doctor's huddled body, the shadowy figure searched quickly through his pockets, found and took the remaining phial of Vraxoin, and hurried from the room.

4

Monster in the Fog

There was an ante-room to the *Empress*'s sickbay, a small, comfortably furnished area, with a window giving on to the operating theatre itself. Rigg was gazing through that window now, watching a team of medics working on Secker's unconscious body, cleaning and sealing the terrible wounds, giving an emergency blood transfusion, using everything that medical skills and up-to-date equipment could provide to preserve the weakly flickering life. Something about the desperate urgency of their movements told Rigg that it wasn't going to be enough.

As he turned away, Della and Tryst hurried into the room. Della glanced through the window, and looked hurriedly away. 'We got your message, Captain. What happened to him?'

'Somebody – or some*thing* – attacked him.'

'It's horrible,' said Della. 'Why was he attacked?'

'I don't know,' growled Rigg.

'It's a terrible business, of course,' said Tryst fussily. 'But I fail to see why this problem concerns us.'

'Then take a look through there, Professor. Look at those wounds.'

Tryst went over to the window and looked through at the silent figure on the operating table. He studied it for a moment, his face impassive. 'Where did this happen?'

'Below the shuttle bay – he seems to have wandered into one of the matter interfaces.'

Tryst turned away from the window. 'Then that is the answer. Who knows what energy-forces may exist in such an unstable zone?'

'You saw the marks on the body,' said Rigg steadily. 'They look to me as if they were made by claws. You didn't bring any *live* specimens on board my ship, did you, Professor?'

'No, Captain, I did not. I can assure you all my specimens are in the form of laser crystal recordings and are utterly harmless.'

'They'd better be.'

A white-coated figure came through the door of the operating room. Rigg looked up eagerly. 'Well?'

The medic shook his head. 'We were too late. He'd lost too much blood.' He paused. 'We might have been able to save him in spite of that – but his system appears to have been weakened by some kind of addictive drug.'

Tired of waiting for the Doctor, Romana went to look for him and ran into K9, who was on precisely the same errand, using his sensors to detect the Doctor's whereabouts.

As they moved along the corridor to the luggage room, K9 said, 'This way, Mistress. Detection of Doctor's presence now confirmed.'

'How far away?'

'Approximately seven metres and closing.'

He led her along the corridor, into the luggage area and straight up to the Doctor's unconscious body.

Romana knelt beside him. 'Doctor!'

She shook him gently. The Doctor moaned and stirred. Relieved to find him alive, Romana said, 'Doctor, wake up! What happened to you?'

The Doctor sat up and groaned, clutching his

aching head. 'I was bushwacked!'

Romana didn't know what he was talking about. 'You were what?'

Neither did K9. 'Expression unfamiliar. Please repeat.'

The Doctor groaned and struggled to his feet. 'Bushwacked,' he repeated indignantly.

K9 whirred and clicked as he searched through his data banks. 'Bushwacked!' he announced with a beep of satisfaction. 'The Doctor has been the victim of a cowardly attack by person or persons unknown.'

The Doctor reached into the pocket where he'd put the phial of Vraxoin. 'It's gone!'

'Something stolen?' asked Romana.

'Some Vraxoin I found. Someone aboard this ship is smuggling drugs.'

'Vraxoin!' Romana was horrified. 'I thought that had been stamped out long ago. Only – they never found the source, did they?'

'No, they didn't. The secret was supposed to have died with the last of the smugglers. Now it looks as if someone's rediscovered it.'

Dymond was pacing up and down impatiently. 'Well, where is this Doctor then? He comes up with a marvellous idea to separate the ships, fiddles about endlessly, and now he's disappeared!'

'Don't tell me your troubles,' said Rigg sourly. 'I've got problems of my own – including a dead navigator. The Doctor's going to cut his way into the power room – which means I'll have a gaping hole in my ship to explain.'

'Well, whatever he's going to do, I wish he'd get on with it,' grumbled Dymond. 'I've got a schedule to keep, you know!'

'So have I,' snarled Rigg, and marched out of the control room.

The Doctor, Romana and K9 were walking along the corridor from the luggage area. As they reached the lift, Romana said, 'Doctor, that machine of Tryst's, the CET machine.'

'What about it?'

'It doesn't just take three-dimensional recordings, does it?'

The Doctor said, 'No, it doesn't. The animals themselves are converted into magnetic signals, together with their surrounding habitats.'

'So he's left bare patches on all the planets he's visited?'

'That's right. The CET machine is no more than an electronic zoo. For cages, read laser crystals. Either way, the animals are trapped inside.'

'Are we sure of that, Doctor?'

'What do you mean?'

'Well, you saw how primitive that device was. Now that the ship is full of these unstable matter zones ... The whole thing gives me the creeps. Suppose something got out of the machine and attacked Secker?'

'*Killed* Secker,' corrected a grim voice behind them. 'He's dead, they couldn't save him.'

Rigg had come up behind them.

'Pity,' said the Doctor thoughtfully. 'He might have been able to tell us what attacked him. You've no idea what it was?'

Rigg shook his head. 'I had a word with Tryst, but he couldn't help either. He swears that machine of his is perfectly safe.'

'Oh, does he? I think you'd better go and take a look at it, Romana. If you're not convinced it's safe, close it down.'

'What are you going to do?'

'Separate the ships – I hope! Come along, Captain, let's try and work our way round to the power unit.'

The VIP lounge was empty when Romana appeared. Thankful she wouldn't have to argue with Tryst, she went over to the CET machine and switched it on.

Once again the sinisterly beautiful jungle landscape of the planet called Eden replaced the opposite wall. It seemed later now and the orange sky was darkening. The croaking of some frog-like nocturnal creatures mingled with the other sounds of the jungle. As Romana stared in fascination, the landscape seemed to exert a hypnotic power, drawing her closer and closer.

It seemed almost as if by taking a few more steps she would actually be *inside* the jungle. Though that was ridiculous, of course. The scene before her was only a three-dimensional projection of the miniaturised landscape inside the laser crystal.

Suddenly, astonishingly, a bright-winged insect like a jewelled moth, fluttered out of the projection and touched her neck.

Romana felt the tiniest of pricks, and sudden drowsiness flooded over her. A tide of darkness swept up and overwhelmed her, and she sank unconscious to the floor.

The jewelled creature fluttered about the lounge for a moment or two, then vanished back inside the projection.

Romana lay still as death on the floor. Above her the nightscape of Eden grew steadily darker. Somewhere in the dense vegetation, something moved ...

After much travelling along corridors and through service tunnels, Rigg came to a halt before a ribbed steel bulkhead. 'Here you are, Doctor, this is the best we can do. We could go further along, but I don't want to damage the air seal, or weaken the hull by cutting through a stress-point.'

'I'm sure K9 will be careful,' said the Doctor soothingly. Won't you, K9?'

'Affirmative, Master!' K9 scanned the steel wall ahead of him. 'Sensors indicate that this would be a most suitable section.'

'Good. Make the gap as big as you can without weakening the hull, will you?'

'Affirmative, Master,' said K9 again. 'The aperture will be 4.63 square metres in size.'

Rigg looked on in astonishment as K9 extruded his blaster, concentrated the beam, and began cutting a fine line through the steel of the bulkhead. 'Very handy, that machine of yours, Doctor.'

'Machine? K9's much more than a mere machine. He's saved my life on many occasions. He even beat me at chess – once!'

The Doctor and Rigg watched K9 cut a window-shaped opening in the steel bulkhead. When the four sides of the oblong were complete, K9 glided to one side. 'The panel is free, Master. It needs only to be lifted away.'

'Right, Doctor, give me a hand,' said Rigg eagerly.

Grasping the ribbed steel projections, the Doctor and Rigg lifted the loose section and lowered it to the ground.

A large, oblong gap was left in the bulkhead. But there was no power unit to be seen on the other side.

Instead the gap was filled with a blue mist, not frozen but swirling eerily.

The Doctor moved forward in fascination. 'We seem to have cut into an interface ...'

40

Suddenly a burning-eyed monster lurched out of the fog, growling ferociously and slashing at him with savage claws.

5

Drugged

With a yell of alarm, the Doctor sprang back.

Luckily for him, the monster was a good deal bigger than the gap, so much so that only its head and shoulders could get through.

Safe, at least for the moment, the Doctor had time to study the creature. The boar-like head had a curiously flattened nose-structure; the huge bulging eyes were a luminous green; and the creature was covered with thick, shaggy fur. Most terrifying of all were the rows of drooling fangs and the massive paws ending in razor-sharp claws. It was all too clear what had caused those terrible wounds on Secker's body.

The monster gave a savage roar and made a determined effort to squeeze the rest of itself through the gap. The Doctor decided to defer further scientific study and shouted, 'K9! Quick, K9!' Raising his head, K9 fired a rapid blast. The monster gave a scream of rage and pain, and disappeared backwards through the gap.

'What the devil was that, Doctor?' asked Rigg amazedly.

'I haven't the slightest idea!'

'And how, in the name of all the suns, did it get onto my ship? First this freak collision, now there's a monster roaming about. The whole thing's totally inexplicable.'

'Nonsense. Nothing's inexplicable,' said the Doctor firmly.

'Then how do you explain it?'

The Doctor thought hard, then shrugged. 'I can't. For the moment at least, it seems to be – inexplicable! Come on, we'd better put the panel back. I'm afraid you'll have to reweld it, K9.'

The Doctor and Rigg lifted the panel back in place. K9 extruded his laser and began rewelding the panel he had just cut away.

'Did you see those claws,' asked Rigg with a shudder. 'That must be what killed Secker.'

'It seems very probable. Though as a matter of fact, Secker was as good as dead already.'

'What do you mean?'

'Secker was taking Vraxoin.' The Doctor looked hard at Rigg, studying his reaction.

Rigg gave a gasp of what looked like quite genuine horror. 'The medic said his system had been weakened by some drug ... So that's why he died.'

'That's right. And unless we find out what's going on here, a lot of other people will die as well.'

Leaving K9 to finish his welding job, the Doctor and Rigg made their way back to the bridge.

Rigg was still brooding over the Doctor's news. 'None of my passengers could have brought Vraxoin on board, I can promise you that.'

'What about the other ship – Captain Dymond's survey vessel?'

'We can soon find out. I'll check it with the scanners. I'll re-scan this ship as well. We've got to find that Vrax, Doctor, it's bad stuff.'

'Bad stuff?' said the Doctor, apalled. 'It's the worst! I've seen whole planets ruined by Vraxoin – while the smugglers made a fortune.'

Rigg nodded shrewdly. 'Your people knew it would be on board, did they?'

'My people?'

'Come on, Doctor, I know who you are now. You're a narc.'

'A what?'

'You're working for the Intergalactic Narcotics Bureau.'

'No, I'm not, I'm just the Doctor. I don't work for anybody.'

Rigg shrugged. 'All right, have it your way. But everybody works for somebody.'

It was clear that Rigg was far from convinced by the Doctor's denials. The Doctor opened his mouth to protest further, and then closed it again. It was as good a role as any, and perhaps it would be easier to let Rigg go on thinking he was some kind of Intergalactic Secret Agent.

They went into the control room and Rigg marched straight over to the scanner screen. The Doctor watched as he flashed up one computerised diagram after another: first a general view of the two ships locked together; then more detailed charts of each ship, section by section.

Finally Rigg switched off the scanner and sat back. 'Well, that's it, Doctor. There's no Vrax on board my ship – or on Dymond's either.'

'You've checked the whole of both ships?'

'You saw me. Every nook and cranny.'

'Secker kept his supply in a locker in the luggage section. I took what was left out of the drawer myself – then someone stunned me and took it away from me.'

'Who?'

'Who indeed? Is there any possible defence against this scanner – some way the Vrax could be shielded so we wouldn't find it?'

'None that I know of,' said Rigg dubiously. 'Mind you, I suppose it's possible. But it would have to be

44

just a very small quantity of the stuff. Listen, Doctor, I know this smuggling's a very serious business, but it isn't really the most pressing of my problems.'

'You want to get the ships separated?'

'Yes, Doctor,' said Rigg patiently. 'But how are we going to do it, if we can't get through to the power unit?'

'There might be a way,' said the Doctor thoughtfully. 'If we used *my* ship.'

'Your ship? Where is your ship anyway?'

'Oh, around,' said the Doctor vaguely.

Rigg gave him a suspicious look. 'There you go again – more mysteries. How do I know I can trust you?'

'Or I you?'

'That's hardly the point.'

'Isn't it? Who's helping whom?'

Rigg sighed, defeated. 'All right, Doctor, what do you want me to do?'

'Stay here until you hear from me. Then when I give the word, get Dymond to put his ship on full power.' Rigg started to object. The Doctor said, 'Just trust me, Captain,' and hurried from the control room.

Romana lay unconscious on the floor of the VIP lounge. Somebody stood looking down at her – somebody who found Romana's presence a problem, and was wondering what to do about it. At the sound of footsteps in the corridor outside, the somebody darted into the alcove that held the food-and-drink dispenser.

Della came into the room, saw Romana stretched out and knelt at her side. 'Romana! Romana are you all right?'

Romana opened her eyes. 'I don't know.' She struggled into a sitting position. 'Yes, I think so.'

Della helped her to her feet and led her over to a couch. 'What happened?'

'I'm not sure, I must have fainted. No, wait a minute ...' Romana touched a finger to a tiny sore spot on her neck. 'Something came out of the picture and touched my neck. A kind of jewelled insect.'

Della's eyes widened. 'A somno-moth!'

'What?'

'There's something we called a somno-moth on Eden. It renders its victims unconscious with a mild narcotic, then takes a drop or two of blood. Harmless really, more of a nuisance than anything else.' Della shook her head decisively. 'But that's ridiculous,' she went on. 'There's no way that the moth could have got out of the projection.'

'I was certainly watching the Eden projection when it happened.' Romana looked at the wall. 'It isn't on any more. Did you switch it off?'

'No, it was off when I came in. I asked you not to put the Eden projection on any more.'

'*You* said *you* didn't like to see it,' corrected Romana. 'Since I was alone, I thought I'd take another look. Besides, you assured me the machine was perfectly safe, didn't you? Is it safe?'

'Of course it is.' Della jumped to her feet. 'Let me get you something to drink, you still look quite pale.'

Della hurried over to the dispenser, studied the computerised controls and dialled. The machine ejected a plasti-crystal tumbler, and filled it with a sparkling golden fluid.

Captain Rigg came into the VIP lounge and hurried over to the dispenser. 'That looks good, Della. What is it?'

Della turned. 'Just a fruit cordial. It's for Romana, she fainted.'

'Fainted? What's the matter with her?'

'Oh, nothing,' said Della quickly. 'Warp sickness probably. She's all right now.'

While they were talking, a hand came from behind the dispenser, tipped a phial of grey powder into the cordial, and disappeared behind the machine. The fine grey powder dissolved instantly, leaving no trace.

'Can I dial you a drink, Captain?' asked Della.

'I'm in a bit of a rush, actually, Della. Mind if I just take this one?' Without waiting for a reply, Rigg picked up the tumbler and hurried out.

Della turned back to the machine, pressed the repeat button, and watched as the dispenser produced another tumbler and filled it up. She picked up the glass of cordial and carried it over to Romana.

K9 waited patiently outside the TARDIS until the Doctor emerged carrying a piece of equipment that looked very like a kind of laser cannon. In fact it was part of the dematerialisation circuit of the TARDIS. A long lead trailed from the demat gun back into the TARDIS itself.

The Doctor set up the contraption in the corridor, aiming it carefully at the wall as if lining up on an invisible target.

K9 stood watching, his head cocked sceptically. 'I predict only sixty per cent chance of success for this scheme, Master.'

The Doctor straightened up. 'Why do you always have to look on the black side, K9? Here I am trying to solve the problem with a brilliant bit of lateral thinking, and you have to spoil things with logic. If we use the TARDIS to boost the dematerialisation process—'

'Localised power is liable to be deficient, owing to

damage to power units,' said K9 dogmatically.

· 'That's why we may need to use the TARDIS dematerialisation circuits as a booster.'

'Scheme is unprecedented and extremely hazardous. I can predict ...'

'Yes, I know, sixty per cent! I still think it's worth a try. So stop grumbling, K9. Let's go and find Romana, and tell her what's going on.'

Captain Dymond's face glared indignantly out of the visi-screen on the *Empress*'s bridge. 'How much longer, Captain Rigg? I've got to be away soon, or I'll lose my contract. I hope you realise that this is all your fault? You were the one who was off course.'

Rigg took a sip of his cordial and grinned at Tryst, who stood looking curiously over his shoulder. 'What if I was? You shouldn't even have been in the same sector!'

'Please, gentlemen,' said Tryst diplomatically. 'Blaming each other will help no one. Since the Doctor is the only one with a constructive plan, you must do all you can to help him.'

Rigg yawned. The strangest feeling of well-being was flooding over him. Despite the crisis, he felt that everything was really all right, couldn't be better in fact. 'The Doctor,' he jeered. 'What do we know about him, eh? He's got some bee in his bonnet about drug smuggling! I ask you – drug smuggling – on my ship!'

'The Doctor really has such suspicions?'

'Yes, and that's all they are. Suspicions!' said Rigg truculently. 'No evidence, no evidence at all. Not a trace of drugs anywhere on my ship, or on Dymond's.' Rigg drained his cordial. 'So that's the least of our worries!'

His voice was becoming slightly slurred.

'The least of our worries,' he repeated and slouched back in his seat.

Tryst looked at him in sudden alarm. There was something very wrong with Captain Rigg.

6

The Fugitive

The Doctor, watched by a now-recovered Romana, was examining the CET machine. 'And you're sure that the insect that attacked you came out of the projection?'

'Quite sure.'

'And so did the thing that killed Secker. You were right about this machine, Romana, it is unstable. Both of those creatures escaped from this electronic zoo here. I wonder which projection they came from?'

'The insect came from a planet called Eden —' said Romana. She broke off as Tryst came into the lounge.

He frowned as he saw the Doctor examining his beloved machine, but managed to change his expression to a rather unconvincing smile. 'Ah, there you are, Doctor! I'm delighted that you take such an interest in my CET machine.'

'I find it absolutely amazing,' said the Doctor solemnly.

'It is rather impressive, isn't it?'

The Doctor's voice hardened. 'I find it amazing that you go on using a machine like this when it's so primitive. The whole thing's utterly unstable.'

'Naturally you have a right to your opinion, Doctor,' said Tryst stiffly.

'I have a right to go on living too — and this machine makes me very nervous.'

'But what do you think is so wrong? Which parts are unreliable?'

The Doctor took a deep breath. 'Well, at a rough guess I'd say the spatial integrator, the transmutational oscillator, the hologistic retention circuit ... need I go on? And as for the dimensional osmosis damper ...'

'The dimen-what?'

The Doctor was horrified. 'You mean you haven't even got a dimensional osmosis damper? Professor, you don't realize what dangers ...'

'Personally I feel that you are exaggerating, Doctor,' said Tryst. 'However, I've decided to turn off the machine and I shan't use it again until I've made a full check. I'll close it down right away.'

'I'm very glad to hear you say that.'

'By the way, I have a message for you, Doctor. They are ready to begin the separation of the ships. Captain Dymond and Captain Rigg are waiting for you.'

The Doctor headed for the door. 'I'm on my way. Come on, Romana, I'll need you in the TARDIS to operate the demat controls. Don't forget to switch that machine off, Professor Tryst!'

The Doctor and Romana hurried out, K9 gliding behind them.

Tryst watched them go, then turned back to his CET machine. Finally he reached out and turned it off, watching sadly as the glowing red crystal went dark.

'You know what, Dymond?' said Rigg suddenly. 'My *Empress* has *eaten* your little ship. Swallowed it up!' He giggled.

Dymond scowled angrily from the screen. 'I don't see why you find it so funny. You could lose your captaincy over this.'

Rigg laughed. 'I know! That's what's so funny!'

The Doctor and K9 came onto the bridge. 'Ready to try again, everyone?' He looked at the visi-screen. 'Captain Dymond, I want you to be ready to put your ship on full thrust the minute I give the word.'

'All right, Doctor, I'm ready.'

Rigg smiled as if the whole thing was some enormous joke. 'And where will you be, Doctor?'

'Here, if that's all right with you. Romana's in my ship, so I can direct the operation from here.'

Rigg waved his hands expansively. 'Certainly, Doctor, be my guest!'

'Thank you.' Taking Rigg at his word, the Doctor leaned forward and stabbed controls on the communication unit. Romana's face appeared on another monitor screen. 'Everything ready, Romana?'

'Ready, Doctor.'

'Good, then we're only waiting for Dymond. K9?'

'Master?'

'Maybe you'd better go and monitor the operation from one of the matter interfaces.'

'Affirmative, Master.' Obediently K9 glided out – but as he left he was muttering obstinately. 'Probability of success only sixty per cent, owing to deficiency in localised energy sources ...'

Dymond's face reappeared on the screen. 'I've run up the engines – ready when you are, Doctor.'

'Right, Captain Rigg, start the power build-up.'

Astonishingly Rigg said, 'Oh, you do it, Doctor. I don't feel well.' He got up and stumbled out of the control room.

The Doctor looked after him in concern – but there was no time to investigate. He slipped into Rigg's command chair, studied the controls, then began running up the power. 'All right, Romana, stand by ...'

K9 glided along the corridors until he reached a barrier of frozen fog, the matter interface where the realities of the two ships merged. He could hear the throbbing of the ship's engines.

Suddenly the fog cleared and the corridor ahead became normal. It seemed that the Doctor's scheme had worked – the ships were separating. Sensors alert K9 glided cautiously forward.

Suddenly fog began forming around him as the freak conditions reasserted themselves. K9 was trapped in an unstable zone. It was too far to go back, but ahead there was a section of clear corridor, normal space. With a final effort K9 glided forward, and found himself on the far side of the barrier. Cautiously K9 moved forward. He was just outside a door marked 'POWER UNIT'. K9 sent out an energy signal that triggered the remote control. The door slid open and he went inside.

On the bridge the Doctor was shouting, 'What's the matter Dymond? Why are you reducing power?'

'I've got to, Doctor. My whole ship's breaking up.'

'Don't lose your nerve now, man. Boost the power again. We were almost there.'

'It's no use, Doctor. The ship won't take the stress.'

The roar of the *Hecate*'s motors dwindled and then died away. The Doctor switched off the *Empress*'s power and stood up, 'Switch off the booster, will you, Romana? I'm going to look for K9, he's taking some readings for me. If I can work out the stress-readings, maybe we can persuade Dymond to have another go.'

The Doctor went out of the control room and made his way to the nearest matter interface. There was no sign of K9. He studied the blurred area thoughtfully. 'Well, he didn't turn back, or I'd have met him on the way. He must have slipped right through during the partial dematerialisation. There's a clever dog!'

The Doctor heard a door close behind him. He turned and saw a figure in space coveralls and goggles moving off down the corridor. 'Excuse me,' called the Doctor. 'Have you seen any sign of –' Suddenly the Doctor realised – this was the man who had ambushed him.

At the sound of the Doctor's voice, the figure spun round in alarm and ran off down the corridor.

Instinctively the Doctor ran after it. 'Hey, stop!'

He ran down the corridor, turned a corner and came to a lift. Its doors were just closing. The Doctor dashed up to the lift, but the sliding doors closed in his face. The Doctor checked the indicator and saw that the lift was going down. Glancing round, he saw a door marked 'STAIRS' and headed for it at a run.

The Doctor rattled down a steep metal staircase, through the door at the bottom and out into the lower-level corridor – just in time to see his quarry disappearing through a set of double doors at the far end. The Doctor hurried after him – and found himself in what he realised must be the tourist passenger section of the cruise liner. He could see row upon row of reclining seats, in which space-coveralled and goggled passengers were dozing and chatting, waiting for the voyage to come to an end.

As soon as the Doctor appeared, he was met with a babble of questions.

'Why has there been a delay?'

'What's going on here?'

'When are we going to land, we've been waiting for ages?'

'Is there anything wrong?'

'I'm looking for a man dressed in coveralls and

goggles like you,' shouted the Doctor. 'Which way did he go?'

'There he is – down there,' said a passenger, and the Doctor saw a figure hurrying down the long centre aisle.

Brushing aside the passengers, the Doctor hurried in pursuit.

He went through another passenger section, then another, and yet another. Just as he was gaining on the hurrying figure, a large and angry female passenger blocked his way. 'What's the meaning of all this delay? When are we going to land on Azure?'

'Please, Madam, let me by. We're doing all we can, I promise you.'.

'And what *are* you doing exactly? I demand to know.'

The Doctor took a crumpled paper bag from his pocket, and stopped the woman's mouth with a sweet. 'Here, have a jelly baby – and don't forget to brush your teeth!' Squeezing past the irate woman, the Doctor hurried on his way.

But the delay had cost him time. The hurrying figure was almost out of sight. This was the last of the passenger sections and, as the Doctor shot out of the doors, he saw yet another lift, its door closing against him. This time the indicator showed that the lift was moving upwards.

A second lift stood beside the first, doors open. The Doctor leaped inside and stabbed at the controls. The doors closed, the lift rose smoothly, the doors opened again, and the Doctor sprang out into the corridor in time to see the man he was after hurrying down the corridor. 'Stop!' yelled the Doctor. The man broke into a run and vanished around the corner.

The Doctor ran after him, turned the corner – and

found the way ahead blocked by a wall of frozen fog. They had reached another interface.

The figure drew a blaster from beneath its coveralls and turned round at bay.

The Doctor moved cautiously forward. 'I only wanted a word with you whoever you are. If I'm not mistaken you took something from my pocket a while ago, and I'd like it back.'

The figure whirled round and plunged into the fog.

The Doctor hesitated a moment – and then ran after him. He found himself in a strange, blurred, nightmarish region, where reality was wrenched and distorted. He seemed to be nowhere, and yet in several places at once. He struggled forward with immense effort, as though the air had solidified. Somewhere ahead, he glimpsed the blurred figure of the man he was hunting.

The Doctor struggled onwards.

Sublimely indifferent to the fate of his ship, Captain Rigg sprawled on one of the couches in the VIP lounge, a drink in his hand. Romana and Tryst were watching him in concern.

'Little ships inside big ships,' said Rigg suddenly. 'Like ships in bottles – or like those sets of Russian dolls, one inside the other. Remember them?'

'Yes, I do actually,' said Romana. 'I don't suppose the people who made them realised they were making a kind of primitive model of the universe.'

Rigg grinned foolishly at her. 'Whassat you say?'

Professor Tryst cleared his throat. 'I don't think the Captain is in the mood to discuss philosophy at the moment. Can I get you anything from the dispenser, Captain? A caffeine capsule, perhaps?'

Rigg waved the offer away. 'No! Let's talk about life – while I wait for my dismissal and execution! Gross dereliction of duty ... and you know what? I couldn't care less!'

'You are too pessimistic, Captain,' reproved Tryst. 'There is still a chance the Doctor may succeed.'

'The Doctor! If you ask me, the enigmatic, all-mighty, Mister Fixit Doctor's just failed again – and I don't care about that, either.'

'He hasn't failed yet,' said Romana. 'I think I'd better go and see what he's doing.'

As Romana left, Rigg leaned closer to Tryst, with an expression of drunken cunning. 'Suppose it's them, eh? Suppose they're the ones who are smuggling drugs ...'

Tryst went over to the dispenser and dialled the traditional remedy for Rigg's condition – a cup of strong black coffee. He carried it back over to Rigg. 'Here, this will make you feel better.' As Rigg sipped the coffee, Tryst went on, 'Surely you don't really suspect the Doctor of being a drug smuggler?'

Rigg stared at him in fuddled surprise. 'The Doctor? Of course not, he's a narcotics agent!'

'I see. Then we must give him all the help we can. What about his friend Romana – is she an agent too?'

'What if she is, I don't care. It doesn't matter.' Rigg leaned forward, as if about to share some great secret. 'Don't you see, nothing matters. Nothing matters at all ...'

Still wading through a blurred unreality, the Doctor sprang forward and grappled with the man he was pursuing. They struggled for a moment, and the Doctor snatched a bracelet from the man's wrist. Suddenly a third figure appeared through the fog, charging straight towards them. The Doctor felt the impact of a massive furred body as the creature smashed into them, knocking them apart. There was a savage roar ...

7

The Rescuer

Romana heard the roaring as she turned the corner and came upon the barrier of frozen fog. She stopped in astonishment, listening.

Suddenly a monstrous shaggy figure lurched out of the fog and shambled towards her, green eyes blazing, fangs slavering, great clawed paws slashing the air.

Romana stood petrified with horror, the claws reached out – and another figure appeared from the fog. It was a man in coveralls and goggles, a blaster in his hand. He fired and the monster swung round, focusing on its attacker.

Springing to one side, the man fired again, and yet again. Romana realised that the shots were driving the creature back towards the fog. A final shot, and the creature fled.

The man looked at Romana for a second, as if assuring himself she was unharmed, then turned and vanished into the fog.

Before Romana had fully recovered from these events there came yet another surprise. The Doctor appeared, crawling out of the mist-zone on his hands and knees.

Delightedly Romana ran up to him and helped him to his feet. 'Doctor, are you all right? Some sort of creature came out of there, it was horrible ... We'd better get away from here. There was this man, he drove it off. And what were you doing in there anyway? Oh, come on, Doctor!'

She tried to drag him away, and the Doctor said, 'Stop making such a fuss, Romana. Do you realise I have just come through a matter interface – no mean feat, that! I'm not even sure I'm all here yet.' The Doctor began patting himself, as if to make sure nothing vital was missing.

'You mean you've been right through, from the other side?'

'I most certainly have. Did you see anyone else, before I came out? Fellow in space coveralls and dark goggles?'

Romana nodded. 'He rescued me from the monster, shot at it and drove it off.'

'That was the man I was chasing, the same chap who jumped me in the luggage section.' The Doctor realised he was clutching something in his hand. He examined it, then held it out to Romana. 'Well, at least we know something about him now. That's his radiation bracelet, it came off in the struggle.'

Romana read the lettering across the base of the little plastic strip. '*Volante*'.

'That's right. The name of Tryst's ship. Rigg said that Tryst and Della were the only ones from the expedition to come on board.'

'A stowaway?'

'It's possible. We'd better have a word with Rigg.'

'I wouldn't bother if I were you, Doctor. Rigg's cracked up under the strain. He's drunk.'

The Doctor stared at her. 'He was unwell in the control room – rushed off suddenly – but drunk? Surely not. Rigg's a professional, he'd never drink on duty, particularly at a time like this.'

'Well, he was sitting about in the lounge just now, saying he didn't care about anything and nothing mattered. He just giggles and laughs all the time, and there's a sick grin on his face.'

'It could be drink, of course,' said the Doctor slowly. 'Or it could be something far worse.'

'Vraxoin? But where would he get it from? I thought you said Rigg had checked both ships.'

'He did. But there's one place where Vraxoin wouldn't show up on the scanner – inside the CET machine. That's the only place, Romana.'

'It's an interesting theory, Doctor. How do we test it?'

'By going inside the machine ourselves –'

They turned a corner and found Tryst hurrying towards them.

'Ah, there you are, Doctor, I've been looking for you. Captain Rigg is unwell, he has retired to his quarters. But before he went he told me about this terrible drug business. I believe I may be able to help you.' Tryst moved closer and spoke in a low voice. 'In my opinion the drugs were smuggled on my ship – and I'm pretty sure I know who did it!'

'And who was that?'

'There is really only one possibility – Stott, the third member of my expedition.'

'I thought he'd been killed – on Eden.'

'He was – but he must have passed on the drugs before he died.'

'To whom?'

'Della, of course. They were very close, you know. I made some attempt to question her, but of course she would admit nothing.'

'Perhaps because she's innocent?' suggested Romana acidly. 'How do you know it was her?'

'My dear young lady, who else could it be?'

'This man Stott, for one,' suggested the Doctor. 'Are you quite sure he's dead? I mean, did you actually see the body?'

'He was acting strangely for some time when we

were on Eden – then one day he went into the jungle and disappeared. We searched and found nothing. Why do you ask, Doctor?'

'Well, as a matter of fact –'

A metallic voice from the intercom system interrupted him. 'Will the individual calling himself the Doctor please report to the bridge immediately.'

There was no sign of Captain Rigg when the Doctor and Romana came onto the bridge. Dymond was in the command chair and there were two grim-faced, black-uniformed figures standing beside him. More black-uniformed guards were grouped behind them.

'Ah, there you are, Doctor,' said Dymond. 'This is Officer Fisk, and Officer Costa, of the Azure Customs and Excise Service. I've been telling them all about you, Doctor. They were very interested.'

The Doctor nodded amiably. 'How do you do, gentlemen? Listen, we've got a very serious –'

Officer Fisk, obviously the more senior of the two officials, marched up to the Doctor. Costa, his colleague, moved to stand beside Romana.

'Identity plaque,' snapped Fisk.

'Can't I just tell you about this drug smuggling –'

'Identity plaque, please,' repeated Fisk emotionlessly.

'Listen, somewhere on this ship ...'

'I want to see your identity plaque – now!'

'Yours too, miss,' added Costa.

Romana shook her head. 'I haven't got one.'

'Neither have I,' said the Doctor.

Officer Fisk looked shocked. 'No identi-plaque. That's a serious offence for a start.'

'Someone's smuggling drugs,' yelled the Doctor. 'Drugs! Vraxoin!'

'Names and dates of birth,' droned Fisk.

'How do I know their names and dates of birth? I

haven't even found out who it is yet.'

'*Your* name and date of birth,' said Fisk wearily.

'Look, just call me the Doctor. As for my date of birth, I can never remember. Sometime quite soon, I think.'

'I would advise you not to play the fool with us, sir,' said Fisk heavily.

'Will you please listen to me for a moment. Vraxoin is the most dangerously addictive drug in existence, and there's a supply somewhere on this ship.'

'We'll come to that all in good time, sir.'

'There is no good time,' snapped the Doctor. 'These criminals must be caught –'

'Costa, check these two over,' snapped Fisk.

Costa produced a black scanner rod, attached by a flexi-lead to the power pack in his belt. 'We'll start with you, miss.'

Romana stood glaring at him while he moved the rod up and down the length of her body. 'She's clean, sir.'

'Now the man.'

Costa moved over to the Doctor and repeated the process.

'You're wasting time with all this nonsense,' said the Doctor impatiently. 'Why don't you just –'

A sudden loud bleeping came from the scanner. Costa checked readings on a dial in its handle. 'Vraxoin, sir. Traces of it in his pocket.'

Fisk gave a smile of satisfaction. 'So we've got to catch the criminals, have we, Doctor? You're under arrest.'

The Doctor sighed. 'All right. May I just say one thing?'

'Well?'

'Run for it, Romana,' yelled the Doctor and sprinted for the door. Romana was close behind him and they were out of the room before the astonished excise men could react.

The Doctor had stabbed at the door control in passing. By the time Fisk and Costa realised what had happened, the door was closing in their faces. Fisk hit the door control, waited for the door to reopen, and dashed off in pursuit of the fugitives.

The Doctor and Romana sprinted down the corridors and ducked into the VIP lounge. The Doctor ran to the CET machine and switched it on. 'Quick, Romana, find me Eden.'

While Romana switched the selector, the Doctor ran to the door and locked it, then came back to the machine. 'Quickly, Romana.'

'All right, Doctor, I've got it.' The landscape of Eden sprang into life on the wall. The same dense green jungle, the same eerie cries, the same glowing, orange sky.

There came a sudden hammering on the door and they heard Fisk yelling, 'Open this door. Open up, or we'll blast the lock!'

Romana turned to the Doctor. 'Well, what do we do now?'

'It's time to test that theory of mine. Come on!'

Romana held back. 'No, Doctor, we can't. It's too unstable.'

The crackle of a blaster came from the corridor and the door-lock began to smoke.

'Come on, Romana. We've got to do it!'

'We could get torn apart!'

'We'll have to risk it,' yelled the Doctor. Grabbing Romana's hand, he dragged her into the projection.

The jungle of Eden swallowed them up.

8

Man-eater

The Doctor and Romana plunged headlong into the jungle. By the time they stopped for breath, they were surrounded by dense foliage. Broad-leaved plants and long, trailing vines struggled for space between mighty trees, whose leaves formed an oppressive canopy overhead. Between the tree-tops, there was an occasional glimpse of Eden's lurid, orange sky. The ground underfoot was damp and soggy, the air warm and humid, filled with the cries of night-birds and shrill chirping of insects. Somewhere not far away, something heavy was crashing through the bushes.

The Doctor looked down at Romana, mopping his brow. 'Well, what do you think of Eden?'

'Not much!'

'Neither do I. But we might find a few answers here, all the same.'

Romana looked around. 'Which way shall we go?'

The Doctor pointed at random. 'Let's go east.'

'How do you know that way's east?'

'I don't. So, let's go that way and call it east.

'Why not call it north?'

'All right, we'll call it north.'

'Tell you what, we'll compromise,' said Romana. 'Call it northeast.'

A savage growl came from somewhere too close for comfort.

'Listen,' said the Doctor. 'Whatever direction we

call it, can we please stop talking and get moving?'

They set off through the jungle.

A shaggy green-eyed form watched them from behind a nearby tree, its lips drawn back in a savage snarl.

It was hard-going through the jungle. There was only the faintest of tracks, and they were constantly thrusting plants and bushes aside.

The Doctor led the way, doing his best to clear a path for Romana. After a while they came to a tiny clearing and paused to rest.

Romana leaned wearily against an enormous tree-trunk. 'Doctor, how did you know we could get into the projection?'

'Same way I know I can get into the TARDIS. Our friend Tryst doesn't realise what he's stumbled on with that ramshackle machine of his – at least, I don't think he does.'

'What has he stumbled on?'

'He's managed to create a limited relative dimensional field.' The Doctor swept his arm round in a circle. 'All this is recorded on laser crystal. When it's played back, it's restructured on an intra-dimensional matrix – roughly speaking, that is.'

Romana said thoughtfully, 'And without a dimensional osmosis damper, everything got mixed up together after the accident, and we can just walk straight into the projection.'

'That's right.'

'So presumably anything else can just walk straight out.'

The Doctor nodded. 'And we both saw one of the things that walked out, back on the ship. We'd better keep moving.'

As they set off again, something crashed by in the distance. Romana shivered. 'We wouldn't even be

66

here if it wasn't for those idiotic customs men.'

The Doctor was struggling to thrust aside a particularly stubborn plant. 'Idiots! They're worse than idiots, they're bureaucrats. All they do is tangle people up in red tape, wrap them round and round until they can't move.' Suddenly the Doctor gave a yell of alarm. 'Romana!'

'What's the matter?'

'I can't move!'

Romana forced her way to the Doctor's side, tentacle-like vines coiling around her body. 'Neither can I!' She began struggling wildly.

'No, don't wriggle,' yelled the Doctor. 'Keep as still as you can. The more you struggle, the more it'll think it's dinner time.'

'Dinner time?'

'That's right. This particular plant is a man-eater!'

The tentacles around the Doctor began to tighten, drawing him closer and closer to the centre of the plant.

Romana tried to pull him back, but she herself was tangled in vines and the plant seemed appallingly strong.

'Never mind getting me free,' yelled the Doctor. 'Root!'

'What?'

'The root – thing like a long cable – get hold of it and bring it to me.'

Although Romana's legs were tangled up, her arms were relatively free. She flung herself forwards, grabbed hold of the long cable-like root and heaved it up towards the Doctor. With a frantic lunge, the Doctor grabbed hold of the root. He tried to twist it and break it in his hands, but it was far too tough.

The plant dragged him closer, and a gaping green mouth opened to receive him.

With a last desperate effort, the Doctor sank his teeth into the root-tendril and bit into it savagely. Green liquid spured out like blood, the plant lashed convulsively, and just for a moment the tendrils relaxed their grip beneath the shock.

The Doctor wrenched himself free, grabbing Romana and pulling her after him. 'Are you all right?'

'I think so – let's get away from that thing.'

The Doctor wiped the last traces of green fluid from his lips. 'You know, that thing didn't taste at all bad!'

Giving the still-lashing plant a wide berth, they forced their way on through the jungle.

Before very long, the blundering crashing sounds came again, close behind them this time.

'Something's following us,' whispered Romana.

The crashing came again, this time from in front of them.

'More than one something, by the sound of it,' said the Doctor. Suddenly a huge shaggy figure burst out of the bushes and stood on the trail just in front of them, pawing the air, swinging its head to and fro. Romana saw again the glowing green eyes, the powerful jaws and slavering fangs, the massive paws tipped with razor-sharp claws.

'Don't move,' whispered the Doctor. 'Don't make a sound.'

They froze like statues, scarcely daring to breathe.

After what seemed like a very long time, the creature snarled angrily and blundered off through the jungle.

The Doctor let out a long sigh of relief. 'Right, on we go. Take care –'

They moved on a few more yards – and a second monster crashed out of the jungle. This one was almost on top of them, and there was no doubt that it had seen them.

Throwing back its head it gave a roar of anger, then blundered forward, slashing the air with its claws.

As they turned to run, the crackle of a blaster came from the jungle shadows. With a scream of rage, the creature turned to face the new threat. The blaster fired again, and yet again. Howling with pain and terror, the monster fled, disappearing amongst the bushes.

A figure stepped out of the shadows and came towards them. Peering through the gloom, Romana saw a tall curly-haired man in space coveralls.

As the man walked towards them, the Doctor said, 'You seem to have saved our lives, very kind of you.'

Now that the man was near them, Romana could see that there were fading claw-marks on one side of his face. 'Who are you?'

'My name's Stott.'

The Doctor fished the plastic bracelet from his pocket. 'Stott ... from the *Volante*, am I right? I think this belongs to you.'

Stott took the bracelet and nodded. The Doctor went on, 'I'm the Doctor and this is Romana. We're travellers and –'

'We'd better not stay here,' interrupted Stott. 'I know somewhere safe. Follow me.'

Stott led them through the jungle at a rapid pace, until they reached a plastic survival dome in a clearing.

They went inside and the Doctor looked round approvingly. 'Not bad, not bad at all. I see you've made yourself quite comfortable.'

The survival dome was the usual lightweight structure, made of green plastic with diamond-shaped windows and doors. As the name implied, it contained the basic equipment for survival: bed, table, chair, a store of food and water, a solar-power pack to provide warmth and light. 'How long have you been here?' asked the Doctor.

'Ever since I was left for dead on Eden.'

'What happened?'

'Someone shot me down from behind, left me in the jungle to die. I survived though, managed to crawl back here. Then I got caught up in the Event Transmuter and imprisoned in the projection when Tryst took his samples.'

Romana looked at the scars on his face. 'How did you get those marks?'

'I ran into a Mandrel – one of those things I chased off just now.'

'Did you hear that, Doctor?' said Romana. 'They're called Mandrels.'

'Fascinating,' said the Doctor drily. He turned to Stott. 'What happened next?'

'I thought I was trapped in here for the rest of my life. The hardest thing was being able to look out and see Della.'

'When did you first discover you could get out of the projection?'

'Just after the accident. Something must have gone wrong with the CET machine. The edge of the projection was shimmering. I discovered I could walk straight through it, and found myself on the *Empress*.'

'Why didn't you tell anyone when you realised you could get out? Why did you go sneaking about the ship disguised as a passenger? And why did you stun me and take Secker's Vraxoin?'

'Because of what I am and what I'm doing.' Stott produced an identi-plaque and handed it to the Doctor. 'I'm a Major in the Intelligence Section of the Space Corps, on a special drug-running assignment.'

The Doctor examined the plaque and returned it. 'And you thought I was the one you were after?'

'Well, when I found you by Secker's locker – with Vraxoin in your pocket ...'

'What changed your mind?'

'I overheard you two talking in the lounge.'

Tryst says *you're* the drug smuggler,' said Romana. 'Now he's saying Della's involved as well. He says he didn't realise his machine was being used to transport Vraxoin – if you store it inside a projection on the CET machine, it doesn't show up on a scan.'

'Well, if the Vraxoin's here in the Eden projection, I haven't found it,' said Stott wearily. 'The smugglers will have arranged for a pick-up somewhere along the line. That means they'll have to get the stuff out of the machine and pass it on.'

'Secker must have been working with them,' said the Doctor. 'They made him an addict and paid him off with the drug. He only had a little though – you took the last phial from me.'

'That would have been his personal supply – just a tiny sample. I need to know where the main supply is hidden – and more important, where's the new source?'

The Doctor stood up. 'The first thing to do is to get this projection safely sealed off again – which means we've got to separate the ships. Tell me, can we get out of the projection somewhere near the *Empress*'s power room?'

'Certainly. You can leave the projection at any point in the matter interface.'

'Then let's get moving. Lead the way, Major Stott!'

Stott led them to a place where the jungle ended in a wall of frozen fog. They plunged in and found themselves in the strange slow-motion world of the matter interface. Stott led the way confidently, and after an unmeasurable amount of time they emerged from the blurred zone to find themselves in the power room – facing an astonished K9.

'Look out!' yelled Stott, and reached for his blaster.

'It's all right,' said the Doctor cheerfully. 'This is a friend of mine.'

'What is it?'

'Oh, just a perfectly normal electronic dog. This is Major Stott, K9, he's a friend.'

The Doctor looked round. They were in a long steel chamber, the walls of which were studded with control panels and crammed with dome-shaped reactor housings.

'Now let me see – liquid-hydrogen pump, turbo-pump exhaust, reactor core, pressure shell. All looks simple enough.' The Doctor produced his sonic screwdriver and attacked the main power console.

Romana looked dubiously at him. 'Doctor, do you really think you can get this thing going?'

'Of course I can. I can start anything from a steam engine to a TARDIS. Got a match?'

'Whatever for? It's not gas-fired is it?'

'No, but I need to jam this switch down. Ah, this'll do.' The Doctor fished a wooden toothpick from his pocket, jammed the switch and set to work.

K9 glided up to him. 'During your absence, my sensors detected the presence of alien creatures in this area. Large ferocious beasts of limited intelligence.'

'Mandrels!' exclaimed Romana.

'Name of alien creature noted, Mistress.'

The Doctor looked up from his work. 'You'd better guard the door, K9. How many were there?'

'Five units, Master.'

The Doctor looked worried. 'Five! We'd better

get a move on or they'll be swarming all over the ship!'

'Shouldn't we try to deal with them now, Doctor,' asked Romana.

'As long as the projection is unstable, Mandrels can enter the ship from Eden whenever they like. It'd be like trying to bail out a small boat with a sieve.'

The large and determined woman to whom the Doctor had given a jelly baby was marching along the ship's corridor escorted by an embarrassed young crewman, who was trying to mollify her without success. 'I assure you we're doing everything possible, Madam. The Captain's got an expert to advise him –'

'We should have been on Azure hours ago, young man. My fellow passengers have asked me to represent them and I insist on taking our complaints to the Captain.'

'I'm afraid the Captain's unwell at the moment, Madam. But I assure you we're doing everything possible to get you to Azure –' The crewman talked on, but the large woman refused to listen.

'I insist on seeing the Captain!'

They'd reached the lift by now. Resignedly the crewman pressed the button.

The lift door slid smoothly open – and a Mandrel sprang out, roaring savagely. One slashing blow silenced the complaining woman forever. The crewman was struck down as he turned to run.

With a roar of triumph, the Mandrel lurched off down the corridor.

9

Monster Attack

Captain Rigg lolled back in his command chair, a fixed grin twisting his face. The control room was filled with the blaring of alarms and the monitor screen in front of him showed a scene of panic and horror, as terrified passengers fled the attacking Mandrels.

Officer Costa came running into the control room and stopped in astonishment at the sight of Rigg. 'I take it you're the Captain? What's going on here?'

'Oh, nothing much,' said Rigg airily.

Costa looked in horror at the monitor screen. 'What's happening? What are those things?'

'A judgement,' said Rigg cheerfully. 'A judgement on us all!' And he burst out laughing.

'I'll have you shot for this, Captain,' snarled Costa. Shoving Rigg aside, he leaned over the intercom. 'Bridge here. Emergency! Passengers in section sixty-seven are under attack. Security guards proceed to area sixty-seven immediately.' Costa straightened up. 'I shall be charging you with gross neglect of duty, Captain Rigg. The safety of the passengers should be your first concern, and here you sit looking on while they're attacked and killed.'

'Oh, what does it matter?' said Rigg carelessly. 'They're only tourist passengers after all. What's all the fuss about?'

Costa was too angry to speak.

The Doctor had lifted the cover off the instrument panel and was working on the fine crystal circuitry beneath. Meanwhile Romana was busy tracing the feed lines to the power core. 'Make sure you get the right cable, Romana,' called the Doctor. 'Because if you don't –'

There was a sudden scream from Romana. 'Look out, Doctor! Mandrel!'

She ran out from behind the reactor housing, the massive shaggy form of a Mandrel lumbering behind her.

The Doctor grabbed her hand and they backed away rapidly. 'K9!' yelled the Doctor. 'Quickly, K9!'

The Mandrel roared and charged, green eyes blazing – and K9 glided in from the corridor and blasted it down.

There came a volley of shots from the doorway and Stott appeared, blaster in hand. 'They're coming from both sides, Doctor!'

'You and K9 will have to hold them off between you, I've got to get this job finished. Did you check the cable to the reactor, Romana?'

'Well, I was interrupted, Doctor, but I'm pretty sure it's the right one.'

'Check it again, I need to be absolutely sure!'

Romana hesitated, unwilling to go too close to the dead Mandrel.

The Doctor poked it in the ribs with his foot. It didn't stir. 'It's all right, Romana, it's quite dead!'

'If you say so, Doctor.' Gingerly Romana stepped over the Mandrel's body and disappeared behind the reactor housing. After a moment the Doctor called, 'Was it the right one, Romana?'

'No, I'm sorry, it was the one below.'

'Just as well you made sure, there could have been a rather spectacular explosion.'

Picking up the right cable, the Doctor worked busily for a few minutes, wiring it directly into the control circuitry.

Romana came to join him. 'Are we ready to go yet, Doctor?'

'More or less – but two things need to be done. The power controls on the bridge have to be set at maximum and someone's got to switch on the demat gun in the TARDIS – all at the same time as I start up this nuclear gas-oven here. All clear?'

By now Officer Fisk had joined Costa on the bridge. If possible he was even more angry and outraged than his colleague. 'I am declaring this ship a disaster area, Captain Rigg. I'm assuming command and placing you under arrest for gross dereliction of duty. Take him away, Costa, confine him to his quarters.'

Costa grabbed Rigg by the arm and dragged him from the bridge. Rigg went with him unprotestingly, as if it was all part of an enormous practical joke. 'So I'm under arrest, eh? That's really nice ...'

Fisk turned to Tryst. 'Now then, Professor, we've got to deal with these Mandrels. We must seal them off, hunt them down and destroy them. I shall send down to Azure for heavy-duty blasters.'

'I'd rather they weren't all killed,' protested Tryst. 'Can't you find some other way?'

'Those things are killing people out there! What do you suggest we do with them?'

'Some kind of tranquillising dart perhaps – I have a supply in my stores.'

'We haven't time to pussyfoot around, Professor. You're in enough trouble as it is, I can't see why you concern yourself about the filthy things.'

'The Mandrels are an endangered species as it is. Kill these and there will be very few left.'

'I'm in charge here now, I shall do as I think best,' snapped Fisk.

A panicky voice crackled from the intercom. 'Fuel section to bridge – there are two Mandrels attacking this section!'

'Then kill them!' ordered Fisk. 'Shoot them down!'

'We'll try, sir – but we're afraid of damaging the fuel tanks.'

'Then keep them under surveillance and destroy them as soon as it's safe to do so.' He flicked to another channel. 'Security section – has there been any sign of the Doctor?'

'Negative, Officer Fisk.'

'Pass the word. He's to be arrested on sight. If he offers any resistance, he's to be shot down. That goes for his companion as well.'

There was a moment's silence from the com-unit, then the voice said, 'Shoot them down, sir – just like that.'

'Certainly. They're criminals, aren't they? What else do you do with criminals?'

Professor Tryst looked worriedly at Fisk. It looked very much as if the *Empress*'s new commander was already cracking up under the strain.

At the door of the power unit. the Doctor was issuing final instructions to his companions. 'Stott, can you guide Romana back through the jungle and get her out of the projection near the TARDIS and the bridge?'

'Leave it to me, Doctor.'

'Right. Now I want you to go back the way you came, K9.'

'Negative, Master,' squawked K9 agitatedly. 'It is unsafe to pass through matter interfaces ...'

'Stott and I got through all right. All you need is

a little determination, K9. You can do it.'

'Determination: fixed purpose; firmness of character. Affirmative, Master!'

'That's the idea. Now, when you get through, I want you to go back to the TARDIS. I've set up a demat booster just beside it.' The Doctor produced his soundless dog-whistle. 'When I blow this, you switch on, all right?'

'Affirmative.'

'What about you, Doctor,' asked Romana. 'You're not going to be down here when the power unit comes on, are you? The way you've rigged things up, there'll probably be a radiation leakage at least, and maybe even a localised explosion.'

'Of course I'm not staying here. I shall rig up a little timing device before I go. Could I borrow your watch, Major?'

Scott slipped off his heavy-duty astronaut's watch and handed it over. 'There you are. It's set to ship's time.'

The Doctor looked at the watch. 'Good. I'll give you until 20.25 to get to the bridge and switch the power on. I'll preset my device and get away in good time.'

'What about the Mandrels,' asked Romana. 'You won't have K9 with you, remember.'

'Then I shall have to use my wits, won't I?' The Doctor beamed encouragingly. 'Now, off you go. Watch out for the Mandrels and watch out for those excise men from Azure, Fisk and Costa. I don't think they like us very much at the moment.'

Stott, Romana and K9 hurried off down the corridor. The Doctor checked the time on Stott's watch. It read 20.01.

He hurried back into the power unit and set to work.

As it happened, Fisk was addressing a squad of armed security men on the bridge at that very moment. 'I want this ship searched from top to bottom. If you see the Doctor and his companion, arrest them. If they resist, kill them!'

The squad leader saluted and marched his men away.

Captain Dymond strode down the corridor towards the shuttle bay. He was wearing a space suit, the helmet held under his arm. Professor Tryst was with him and they were talking in low, urgent voices. They stopped outside the airlock. 'We'll just have to see how things develop,' said Tryst. 'I'll be in touch.'

Dymond nodded and went into the airlock, closing the door behind him.

Tryst walked away looking very preoccupied.

Romana and Stott were hurrying through the dense jungle of Eden. Stott lead the way confidently along the narrow overgrown trail.

'Look out!' screamed Romana.

A Mandrel leaped roaring from the jungle.

Stott's blaster was already in his hand and he blasted the monster down with a volley of shots.

As they edged past the body and continued on their way, it occurred to Romana that there couldn't be that many Mandrels left on Eden.

The Doctor was using Stott's watch for the main part of his timing mechanism, wiring it into the circuitry so that it would switch on the antiquated engines at precisely 20.25.

Behind him lay the body of the Mandrel, shot down by K9. In his preoccupation, the Doctor had forgotten that Mandrels are incredibly tough. K9 had fired

only once, while Stott had always fired several times —
it took more than one blast to kill a Mandrel — and
the massive creature just behind the Doctor was be-
ginning to stir ...

As the Doctor worked on, the Mandrel rose slowly
to its hind legs behind him. It raised its paw to
strike ... His work complete, the Doctor straightened
up. 'There we are, all finished with time to spare!'
He was about to put away his sonic screwdriver when
it slipped between his fingers and rattled to the floor.

The Doctor stooped to pick it up, and the razor-
sharp claws of the Mandrel whizzed over his head.

Snatching up the sonic screwdriver, the Doctor
backed away. The Mandrel lumbered after him,
growling angrily.

The Doctor backed to his timing device. His eyes
fixed on the Mandrel, he reached out and switched
it on.

The action seemed to disturb the Mandrel and it
lunged forward with a roar of fury. The Doctor
ducked and the paw missed him by inches — slamming
instead into the centre of the now-live circuit.

As the heavy paw struck it, the circuitry exploded
in a crackle of power and a shower of sparks.

'Oh no!' yelled the Doctor in dismay.

For a moment the heavy body of the Mandrel was
outlined in fire. Then it vanished, collapsing in on
itself, reducing with amazing speed to a pile of dust
on the floor of the power unit.

Astonished, the Doctor stood looking down at the
little heap of grey powder, all that remained of the
once-powerful beast. There was something very
familiar about that dust ...

The Doctor bent down, took a pinch between
finger and thumb, and rubbed it between his fingers.
'Of course — Vraxoin!'

So that was the mysterious source of the drug, thought the Doctor. The Mandrels of Eden. Something in the organic composition of the planet's soil, absorbed into the Mandrel's body, transmuted, rendered up into its final form when the Mandrel was destroyed by intense heat.

'So that's it,' muttered the Doctor. It was satisfying to have at least one mystery solved, but there were more urgent problems.

With frantic speed, the Doctor started work on his shattered timer.

Luckily Stott's watch was still undamaged and, even more amazingly, it was still working.

The dial read 20.15.

The Doctor had exactly ten minutes.

10

The Plotters

The jungle of Eden came to a sudden shimmering end — and Romana found herself looking out into the VIP lounge. She could see Fisk and Costa sitting with drinks at a table near the door.

She turned to Stott. 'Look, I can find my way from here. Will you go back and help the Doctor, he may need you to guide him through.'

Stott hesitated. 'What about those two?'

'I'll manage.'

'Right. Good luck.' Stott disappeared into the jungle.

Romana looked at Fisk and Costa. Their backs were towards her, their heads down over a pile of papers. Choosing her moment, she slipped out of the projection and into the lounge, ducking down behind a couch.

She heard Costa's voice. 'How much longer will we have to stay on board the ship, sir?'

Then Fisk's reply. 'Until the job's over, of course.'

'How many casualties so far, sir?'

There was a rustle of paper. 'Twelve dead, twenty-nine injured. Enough for a small war.' There was something very like satisfaction in Fisk's voice. 'You know what this means, Costa? Promotion! Promotion for both of us. A disaster as big as this — and we'll be the ones who sorted it out and captured the criminals.'

'We haven't exactly done either, yet, sir.'

'Just matter of time. The *Empress*'s crew will deal

with those creatures in the end. As for the criminals, we've got two ready-made culprits, the Doctor and the girl. We'll be the golden boys of the service.'

'We don't actually know they're the criminals, sir.'

'You found traces of Vraxoin in the Doctor's pocket, didn't you? What more do we need? Once I get my hands on them, we'll have a nice quick confession, I'll see to that. Or better still, they'll be shot trying to escape. One thing about dead suspects, they never argue. Come on!'

Romana heard the rustle of papers being gathered up and stowed away. Then came the sound of the two men leaving the lounge.

Romana waited for them to get clear and then slipped out after them.

She managed to reach the control room without being seen and hurried inside. To her relief the bridge was empty. She was heading for the power control console at the far end when suddenly Rigg stumbled on to the bridge. He thrust her aside. 'Tried to lock me up, they did. Me! I soon dealt with their stupid guard, never knew what hit him. I'm still Captain of this ship.'

He glared truculently up at her, face drawn and eyes red-rimmed.

'Listen, Captain Rigg,' said Romana urgently. 'The Doctor's managed to get into the power unit. We're going to try and separate the ships.'

Suddenly she realised that Rigg hadn't been listening to her. He leaned forward. 'Listen, you've got to give me something ... something I need.' His voice was slurred and his eyes completely mad.

Romana backed away. 'Please, Captain, I *must* put full power on.'

Rigg ignored her. 'I must have something, you see. Something for this terrible craving.'

'But I haven't got anything to give you.' '

'Oh yes you have,' whispered Rigg crazily. 'Vraxoin! Someone fed me Vrax, you see, and I'm hooked now, just like Secker was. You and the Doctor are smuggling, aren't you? I know you've got the stuff.'

Romana made her voice sound calm and reasonable. 'Look, Captain, just let me set the controls and I'll help you. You want us to free your ship, don't you?'

'I don't care about the stupid ship, woman. I want something to stop me feeling like this, something to give me that wonderful feeling of happiness again ... You can help, can't you?' Rigg fished a handful of plastic cards out of his pocket. 'I've got plenty of credits, you can have whatever you want.'

Romana thrust him away. 'Just let us get the ships in operation again and we can get you medical help. They can cure you.'

Rigg glared at her with murder in his eyes. '*Why?*' he sobbed. 'Why won't you help me. You've got the stuff. Now, let me have some, or I'll kill you!'

He sprang forward, with his hands reaching for her throat.

'I haven't got any,' gasped Romana. She backed away again. Rigg came after her and forced her into a corner. Romana screamed ...

Suddenly there came the crackle of a blaster from the doorway. Rigg stiffened and fell.

Romana looked up and saw Officer Fisk in the doorway, blaster in his hand. There were two armed security guards beside him.

'Thank you,' gasped Romana. 'I think he would have killed me.'

Fisk nodded to the guards. 'Take him away.' The guards dragged Rigg's body out and Fisk turned his blaster on Romana. 'I shot him down because he was

84

an escaped prisoner. As for his killing you, it wouldn't have mattered much. You're going to die anyway. Now, of course, if you were to make a full confession, things might go easier with you ...'

The Doctor was improvising a complicated electronic lash-up, working against time at incredible speed. Sweat poured down his forehead and splashed onto his hands.

The Doctor mopped his brow with his sleeve and went on working. He glanced at the watch dial. It read 20.23. Less than two minutes to go.

'Look, there's nothing to confess,' said Romana desperately. 'We're not smugglers – the Doctor's trying to put an end to the smuggling.'

'You're smugglers all right, both of you. I heard Rigg asking you for Vraxoin. Drug smuggling is punishable by death on Azure.'

'Whereas bureaucratic murder is rewarded by promotion? I heard you two plotting in the lounge.'

Fisk shrugged. 'I didn't invent the rules – I just enforce them.'

Abandoning argument, Romana headed for the power console.

Fisk raised his blaster. 'Don't touch those controls.'

'You don't understand. The Doctor's in the power unit now. We're going to try to separate the two ships. I've *got* to put the power controls to maximum now or it just won't work.'

'I don't know what you're up to, but I intend to prevent you anyway,' said Fisk with a fine lack of logic. 'I advise you not to move. Touch those controls and I'll shoot!'

Romana reached for the power switch. 'You're going to kill me anyway. What have I got to lose?'

85

In the power unit the Doctor finished work on his timer. Because of the delay, it was now set to go off in just over one minute. The Doctor crossed his fingers, uttered a quick mental prayer, switched on the mechanism, and sprinted for the door.

One eye on the bridge clock, Romana stood with her hand over the power switch.

Fitch levelled his blaster at her head. 'Touch that switch and I'll kill you.'

The bridge clock changed from 20.24 to 20.25.

Romana threw the switch.

In the power unit, the antiquated atomic motors came to life with a roar ...

The Doctor, still running, put the silent whistle to his lips and blew.

Waiting outside the TARDIS, K9 sent out the impulse that switched on the demat booster. It began throbbing with life.

Locked together in space, the two ships began shimmering in and out of dematerialisation ... Slowly, very slowly, they began drawing apart.

All over the ship, reality blurred, twisted and shimmered.

Fisk staggered back, his shot going wild ...

As the Doctor ran along the corridor a blurred zone appeared around him.

He tried desperately to break through, but he seemed trapped – the zone seemed to be stretching, becoming wider and wider. With sudden horror the

Doctor realised that he'd been caught in a matter interface between the separating ships. Unless he could reach the other side, the very molecules of his body would be torn apart.

11

The Secret of the *Hecate*

Separated at last, the space cruiser *Empress* and the sleek survey ship *Hecate* floated serenely side by side, in orbit around the beautiful ocean-planet of Azure.

Groaning, Fisk managed to sit up, raising his blaster. Before he could get up, Romana kicked the weapon neatly from his hands and ran from the bridge.

Cursing and rubbing his hand, Fisk located the gun, picked it up and got dazedly to his feet.

He heard an exultant voice from the monitor screen and saw Dymond's excited face looking out at him. 'He's done it. *Empress*, this is *Hecate*! Full separation has been achieved. There is no damage to report. *Empress* this is *Hecate*, please respond.'

Fisk walked over to the screen. 'All right, Dymond, I can hear you,' he said sourly. 'This is Fisk. Who gave you permission to return to your ship?'

'I came aboard for weapons to help fight those Mandrel things. The ships separated while I was on board. Is there any damage to the *Empress*?'

'Doesn't seem to be.'

'Splendid. Then if you don't mind, Officer Fisk, I'll be on my way. Naturally I won't be pressing any damage claims ...'

The idea of Dymond being free to go about his

business was quite unacceptable to Fisk's bureaucratic mind. 'No, no, no, out of the question. There's the drug smuggling, the escape of the Mandrels, the question of the Doctor. There's bound to be a full enquiry and you'll be needed as a witness.'

'I can't afford any more delay,' protested Dymond furiously. 'I'll lose my contract.'

Frustrated by Romana's escape, Fisk was glad to have someone he could safely bully. 'This is an official warning, Captain Dymond. When this accident occurred, you were in a prohibited area. That makes you liable to a heavy fine at the very least. If you try to leave without my permission, I'll order the coastguard battlecruisers to shoot you down. Do you understand me, Dymond?'

'Yes, Officer Fisk,' said Dymond wearily.

'Good. Then get yourself back on board the *Empress* right away.'

Romana ran up to the door of the TARDIS, where she found K9 looking very pleased with himself. 'Operation one hundred per cent successful, Mistress,' he reported smugly.

'Yes, I know, K9, but I can't find the Doctor. See if you can locate him with your sensors.'

K9 whirred and clicked and revolved solemnly until he had described a full circle. 'I regret, Mistress, no trace of the Doctor can be detected.'

'Well, he must be somewhere. Tell you what, K9, we'll split up and look for him.'

'Affirmative, Mistress.

Romana hunted through the corridors of the *Empress* without success. Everywhere seemed deserted, though once or twice she ducked into hiding as a patrol of armed crewmen hurried by, presumably hunting for the few Mandrels still at large.

She caught sight of a familiar figure at the end of a corridor and hurried after it. It was Della, helping a medic to push a trolley with a wounded passenger into the sickbay.

Romana ran up to her. 'Della, wait! Have you seen the Doctor anywhere?'

'I've been too busy helping with the casualties.' Della looked round, lowering her voice. 'I heard that the excise men ordered him shot on sight – you too, I'm afraid. We'd better go in here.'

They went into the empty ante-room of the sickbay. Through the window they could see teams of medics working on wounded passengers.

Romana said. 'Della, could you bear it if I asked you about Eden?'

'Why?'

'Tryst was hinting that *you* were involved in the drug running. We don't believe him, but it would help if you could tell us what did happen.'

'All right.' Della paused, remembering. 'I spent most of that last day with Stott. We were very close by then, but he was acting strangely. He seemed to want to get rid of me, kept on telling me to go back to the ship. I got the impression he was looking for something.' She shuddered. 'Then it happened. There was a shot from the forest and he fell. Then a Mandrel came out of the jungle and ... I ran. I just couldn't help myself. I was so afraid. I just ran and left him – and the Mandrel killed him.'

'How do you know?'

'Tryst told me. He was out looking for us and he found the body. He showed me a visi-print. It was horrible ...'

Romana put an arm round her shoulders. 'Stott didn't die, Della. He's here, on this ship. He got trapped in the Eden projection.'

Della stared wonderingly at her. 'Where is he? I must see him.'

'Yes, of course – and we must find the Doctor as well!'

The Doctor awoke to find himself in a bare metal corridor, narrower and darker than those on the *Empress*. He got groggily to his feet and found himself outside a cabin door. He went inside.

The cabin, like the corridor, was dark and cramped, with battleship-grey metal walls. Standing by the single porthole was a CET machine, exactly like the one on the *Empress*, except for the laser cannon device clamped to its side.

The Doctor scratched his head. 'An encoder laser. How odd! How very odd!'

The laser was trained out of the cabin's solitary porthole. The Doctor looked out aligning himself along the sights of the laser. Floating just a few metres away was the enormous bulk of the *Empress* – and the laser device was trained precisely on one of the liner's many rows of portholes.

The Doctor sat down on the narrow bunk. It was obvious what had happened. He'd reached the far edge of the blurred zone after all and had emerged in a corridor on Dymond's ship, the *Hecate* – where something strange was going on.

There was a massive computer read-out terminal in the corner. The Doctor went over to examine it – and heard footsteps coming down the corridor.

Quickly the Doctor ducked down into the dark corner behind the big computer console. He heard someone come into the cabin, sit down at the computer terminal keyboard, and switch on the read-out screen. For a minute or two the man sat at the keyboard punching up information. Then with a grunt of satisfaction, he rose and left the cabin.

The Doctor waited a minute or two then came out of his cramped hiding place. He sat down at the keyboard, studied the controls, switched on the read-out screen and punched up 'Repeat'.

Immediately information began to flow across the screen.

'Eden Operation – Budget.'

Beneath were rows and rows of figures.

The display changed. 'Eden Operation – Projected Turnover.' Then more figures, many more of them this time. It was clear that profits were at least a hundred times greater than expenditure. The Eden Operation, whatever it was, was very profitable indeed.

The Doctor switched off the computer and slammed his fist down on the console. 'The profits on human misery,' he muttered savagely.

He heard footsteps again and flattened himself behind the door. This time the footsteps went right by and, looking out, the Doctor saw Dymond going down the corridor in a space suit.

The Doctor tiptoed after him.

He followed Dymond down the narrow corridor into a small bare ante-chamber, on the far side of which was an open airlock door. The Doctor could see through the airlock and into the control cabin of the tiny shuttlecraft beyond.

Dymond stood with his back to the Doctor. He was putting on his helmet and adjusting the seals. The Doctor slipped past him, through the airlock and into the shuttlecraft, and ducked down into the cramped space behind the pilot's seat.

Seconds later there came the clang of the airlock door and the sound of Dymond entering the cabin and settling himself in the pilot's seat. The Doctor heard the roar of the motors, and something else – a strange hissing sound.

He peeped over the edge of the chair and saw Dymond attaching an oxygen lead to the space helmet. With a sudden shock, the Doctor realised that the shuttlecraft was so primitive that the cabin wasn't pressurised. He would be making this journey without benefit of oxygen.

Luckily the trip would be a short one. Calling upon his Time Lord training, the Doctor closed his eyes and went into a trance, suspending his life-processes until the trip was over. The shuttlecraft separated itself from *Hecate* and floated slowly towards the *Empress*.

Fisk studied the approaching shuttlecraft on the monitor screen on the bridge of the *Empress*. He turned to Costa. 'Right, Dymond's on his way back. Any sign of the Doctor?'

'No, sir, they're still searching.'

A voice behind them said. 'I think I may be able to tell you where the Doctor is.'

Fisk turned. 'Professor Tryst! Why didn't you tell me this before?'

Tryst gave a rueful smile. 'I was afraid you wouldn't believe me. You still may not.'

Fisk's voice hardened. 'Then convince me, Professor.'

'I think the Doctor went into the Eden projection.'

'What?'

'The CET machine's image has become a kind of unstable dimensional field. You remember that the projection was there in the lounge when you broke in? It's there now. I have just discovered that someone has sabotaged the controls – the projection cannot be changed, or the machine switched off.'

Della and K9 were waiting outside the TARDIS when Romana arrived. 'Did you find anything?'

Della shook her head. 'Only a Mandrel – and it nearly found me. The crew are still hunting them.'

'Well, the Doctor must be somewhere. What about you, K9?'

'Negative, Mistress. I have scanned the ship and there is no trace –' K9 broke off. 'Correction, Mistress. The Doctor has just come on board. This way, please!'

K9 moved off.

As oxygen hissed into the shuttlecraft cabin, the Doctor opened his eyes and saw Dymond removing his helmet and climbing out of the pilot seat.

Uncoiling his cramped limbs, the Doctor climbed out of his hiding place and left the cabin.

Cautiously he slipped through the airlock and off after Dymond.

12

The Smugglers

On the bridge, Fisk was still grappling with Tryst's new theory. 'If the Doctor did go into this projection, he's got to come out of it sometime. Check the VIP lounge, Costa, I'll join you there in a moment.'

Unholstering his blaster, Costa hurried away. Fisk turned back to Tryst. 'What puzzles me is, why would the Doctor want to go into the projection?'

Tryst shrugged. 'To escape from you, that is one reason. But I believe there is another, more urgent one. My theory is that one of the crew on my expedition, a man called Stott, found a new source of the drug Vraxoin on the planet Eden. He must have placed a supply of the drug inside the projection, and the Doctor has gone to collect it. That is why he came on board in the first place.'

Tryst leaned forward persuasively. 'That is your own brilliant theory, is it not?'

'Yes ... yes, as a matter of fact it is,' said Fisk, who now firmly believed he'd thought up the whole idea. 'But in that case, why did the Doctor bother to separate the ships?'

Tryst shrugged. 'Once the accident had occurred, it provided a useful cover, an ideal way to divert suspicion. After all, the Doctor is a particularly cunning criminal...'

Thanks to K9's sensors, Romana was soon enjoying a joyful reunion with the Doctor. 'But where *were* you Doctor. What happened to you?'

'I got caught up in a matter interface when the ships separated. Luckily I managed to get through it and I ended up on the *Hecate* –'

'Halt! Stay where you are!' Two security guards appeared at the far end of the corridor. A blaster bolt whizzed over their heads.

K9 fired back and a guard fell, stunned.

'Quick, run for it!' shouted the Doctor.

They ran, all except Della. Since she hadn't actually done anything wrong, she saw no reason to run away.

The other security guard hurried up, covering her with his blaster. 'Those two are wanted criminals. What were you doing with them?'

'Oh, just finding out a few things,' said Della coolly.

'You'd better come and tell Officer Fisk all about it. He'll be interested.'

The guard marched Della away.

Satisfied they'd shaken off pursuit, at least for the moment, the Doctor and Romana slowed to a walk as K9 caught up with them.

'Bit uncivil of them waving guns at us like that,' complained the Doctor.

'According to Della, they've got orders to shoot on sight.'

The Doctor didn't seem bothered. 'Tell me, what would you use an encoder laser for?'

'Sending telecom messages. An encoder can carry thousands of them.'

'Could it transmit a CET projection crystal?'

Romana considered. 'Like Tryst's you mean? Yes, theoretically. Why?'

'Because Dymond's got a CET machine on board the *Hecate* – with an encoder laser attachment.'

'So Tryst and Dymond must be the smugglers?'

'It looks like it. The problem will be convincing Fisk, he's convinced it's us. We should have to catch them more or less in the act of transferring Vraxoin.'

'Someone approaching, Master,' warned K9.

The someone was Stott, who was retreating before an attacking Mandrel, firing as he came.

'Stand aside, Stott,' called the Doctor. 'Leave it to K9.'

Stott flattened himself against the wall, K9 fired, and fired again, and the Mandrel fell.

Stott holstered his blaster. 'Nice to see you again, Doctor. What happened to you?'

'Never mind about that now. We've found out who the smugglers are. Dymond is the pick-up man and the smuggler is Tryst himself. The Vraxoin source is on the Eden crystal, as you thought. They're going to transfer it to the *Hecate* by encoder laser.'

'You've actually found the source? I searched for ages. What is it?'

'Roast Mandrel,' said the Doctor solmenly. 'One of them attacked me in the power unit, crashed into a live circuit and got electrocuted. It burned down into a fine grey powder.'

'A powder? You don't mean –'

'Oh yes I do – Vraxoin!'

Stott shook his head in astonishment. 'No wonder I couldn't find the source. And they're actually planning to make the transference between ships with an encoder laser? How are you going to prove it?'

The Doctor smiled. 'I'm going to let them do it!'

The guard marched Della along a corridor towards the bridge, around a corner and straight into a roaming Mandrel.

Della screamed and jumped back, the guard fired

and missed, and the Mandrel struck him down. Della ran along the corridor and into the control room -- where she found Dymond and Tryst, who was just climbing into a space suit taken from one of the lockers on the bridge.

'There's a Mandrel out there,' gasped Della.

'It's all right,' said Tryst soothingly. 'Our friend Dymond has a gun.'

Drawing his blaster, Dymond moved to cover the door.

Suddenly Della realised what Tryst was doing. What's happening? Surely you weren't thinking of leaving the ship? You've got to stay and help the Doctor. He warned you the CET machine was unstable. You've got to help him to get the Mandrels back into the projection.'

'Is that what the Doctor plans to do?'

'Yes, I think so.'

Tryst smiled. 'Then in that case, I shall be right behind him.'

The Doctor was bending over the CET machine in the VIP lounge, replacing the controls he had removed earlier. Just as he finished, Fisk's voice came from behind him. 'Put your hands up, Doctor!'

The Doctor turned. Fisk and Costa were standing in the doorway, armed guards behind them.

The Doctor sighed. 'You're arresting the wrong person, you know.'

Fisk drew his blaster. 'That's enough out of you Doctor. One false move and you'll be shot trying to escape – and personally I'd be just as pleased.'

Another voice said, 'Stop!'

Fisk looked up. To his utter astonishment he saw Stott walk out of the Eden projection into the lounge. 'Who are you?'

Stott tossed him his identity plaque. 'Major Stott, Space Intelligence. The Doctor's helping me. Tryst and Dymond are the ones you want.'

On the bridge, Della was becoming increasingly suspicious. There was something very odd about Tryst's manner. As they talked he went on adjusting his space suit, fastening the seals.

Suddenly Della remembered what the Doctor had told her. 'Professor Tryst – Stott is still alive.'

A very ugly expression came over Tryst's face. 'Alive? He can't be!'

In the doorway, Dymond suddenly swung his gun to cover Della.

Della herself was staring at Tryst with sudden realisation. '*You* fired that shot, didn't you. It was you, that last day on Eden ...'

Tryst seemed to quail before her anger. 'Believe me, I didn't want to do it. He forced me.'

'And *you're* smuggling the Vraxoin. It was you all along.'

'It started just as a temporary measure, Della. To help me with my financial difficulties. The cost of the expeditions was rising all the time, it was bankrupting me. When I stumbled upon the actual source of Vraxoin, the temptation was too great.'

Della was horrified. 'But Vraxoin! A drug that's destroyed people by the millions. How could you?'

'I had to continue my researches,' pleaded Tryst. 'Without me, many of the creatures we found might have become extinct.'

'Don't you think all those addicts becoming extinct is rather more serious?'

'But they had a choice,' explained Tryst earnestly. 'It's their own fault if they choose to become addicted. I didn't force them.'

99

'Like Rigg, I suppose? Did he have a choice?'

'That was most unfortunate. The dose was intended for the girl Romana. She had seen the insect come out of the projection, she could prove it was unstable. I thought if she became confused, unwell, no one would believe her.'

Dymond raised his blaster. 'I'm sorry about this Della – but it's necessary ...'

Della looked at him unbelievingly, scarcely able to realise that he was about to shoot her. Suddenly a Mandrel lurched roaring onto the bridge.

Dymond swung round and fired, hitting it in the shoulder. The Mandrel screamed with rage and returned to the attack.

'Kill it,' shouted Tryst.

Dymond dodged the enraged Mandrel and fired again. 'Kill it? I can't even stop it!'

Seizing her chance, Della ran for the door.

'Tryst, help me,' screamed Dymond.

Tryst drew a blaster from beneath the spacesuit and added his fire to Dymond's. Between them they managed to kill the enraged Mandrel at last.

As it thudded to the ground Tryst looked round. 'Della's gone. Get after her!'

Dymond ran from the bridge and Tryst hurried over to the communications console. Raising his blaster, he wrecked the controls with one long savage burst.

Della ran terror-stricken down the long corridor from the bridge. She turned the corner – and found her way barred by an approaching Mandrel.

She turned and ran back the way she had come – and Dymond appeared at the other end of the corridor. He raised his blaster and fired.

13

Round-up

Clutching her shoulder, Della twisted in the energy-beam of the blaster and fell to the ground.

Romana and K9 appeared from a side corridor and saw Della's fallen body, Dymond at the end of the corridor with the blaster still in his hand.

'After him, K9!' shouted Romana. 'Don't let him get away!'

K9 set off after Dymond while Romana ran to Della's body. Della opened her eyes and moaned.

Suddenly Romana heard the roar of an attacking Mandrel close behind her.

K9 heard it too. Abandoning his pursuit of Dymond, he spun round and glided back to help Romana.

As the creature drew back its paw to strike, a well-aimed blast from K9's laser sent it screaming down the corridor.

'Mission to capture escaping criminal aborted, Mistress,' said K9 apologetically. 'Your protection has a higher priority in my programming.'

'Don't apologise,' gasped Romana. 'That was close!'

'Two metres to be precise, Mistress,' agreed K9

The Doctor came running up the corridor. 'I heard firing. What happened?'

'K9 shot a Mandrel, and Dymond shot Della,' explained Romana.

The Doctor knelt to examine Della. 'She'll be all

right. The range must have been too great, she's only stunned.' He straightened up. 'Callous wretches, Dymond *and* Tryst. Still, we'll see they get what they deserve. They'll be making the energy transfer any minute now.'

Dymond and Tryst were running frantically for the shuttle bay. Suddenly an announcement blared from the ship's loudspeakers. 'All security personnel! Locate and detain Pilot Dymond and passenger Tryst. They may be attempting to leave the ship. Previous orders regarding the Doctor and his companion are now cancelled.'

'They're on to us,' said Tryst. 'It's come sooner than I thought.'

Dymond said, 'We'd better get a move on. Even if we get clear, they'll have interceptor craft after us.'

Tryst smiled. 'I doubt that. I smashed the communicator. They're cut off from Azure control.'

They hurried into the shuttle bay.

Stott and Fisk were on the bridge, surveying the wrecked communication console.

'There's no way I can call up help now,' said Fisk. 'If we don't get them before they leave the ship, we've lost them!'

'We could chase them in the *Empress*,' suggested Stott.

'With no pilot, no navigator, and a damaged power unit? Could you fly her?'

Stott shook his head.

The Doctor, Romana and K9 came onto the bridge. 'Once more into the breach, gentlemen,' said the Doctor cheerily. 'What's happened, why such long faces?'

'Tryst and Dymond have got away,' said Stott gloomily.

The Doctor sat down at the controls. 'They won't go without the Eden crystal,' he said confidently. 'That gives us a little time.'

'To do what?'

'Well, now that the ships are separated, we can stabilise the projection – which means we can clear the marauding menagerie of Mandrels back where they came from. Which is exactly where Tryst and Dymond want them, incidentally.'

'So why are we giving them what they want?'

The Doctor looked at him in surprise. 'We've got to bait the hook first, my dear chap. How else will we catch the fish? Now, let's see how your security chaps are getting on, shall we?"

The shuttlecraft left the *Empress* and floated towards the *Hecate*. Dymond and Tryst were on their way.

On board the *Empress*, operation Mandrel was under way. A thorough check established that there were only about half a dozen of the creatures still roaming the ship. The rest had been dealt with by a combination of Fisk's security guards, armed crewmen, and a number of passengers who had insisted on being given arms.

Now the surviving Mandrels were being driven towards the VIP lounge by Stott and a squad of security guards. On the Doctor's instructions, the blasters were set to stun, and were being used to prod the snarling Mandrels along the corridors.

'Keep them moving,' ordered Stott. 'They're more dangerous in a group. We should join up with Fisk and his squad soon.'

At the next junction they encountered Fisk, more

guards, and several more angry Mandrels. Soon the combined group of Mandrels, about a dozen in all, was being herded down the corridor to the VIP lounge.

The Doctor came down the corridor to meet them. 'Well done. This way, gentlemen, this way!'

Suddenly a kind of group madness seemed to seize the Mandrels. Roaring and snarling, they turned on their captors, slashing at them with their ferocious claws, ignoring the stinging of the blasters.

The panic-stricken security guards fell back.

'We can't hold them, Doctor!' shouted Stott.

The corridor was suddenly filled with a mob of shouting guards and roaring, snarling Mandrels.

The Doctor surveyed the scene in horror. 'Oh no!' Suddenly he had an inspiration. Fishing out his dog-whistle, he put it to his lips and began playing a silent tune.

Whatever he was playing, and whatever strange key and unknown frequency he was playing it in, the result was extraordinary, at least as far as the Mandrels were concerned.

Suddenly docile, they stopped their savage attack and cocked their great shaggy heads as if listening to the sweetest music.

The howls and snarls were replaced by a low contented growling that might have been purring.

The astonished guards fell back and the Mandrels lurched towards the Doctor, following him meekly down the corridor, across the VIP lounge and into the Eden projection, where it glowed on the wall.

Stott, Romana and all the others watched in astonishment as the Doctor and his strange flock vanished into the jungle.

There was a moment of total silence.

Suddenly there came a savage Mandrel roar, and

the Doctor shot out of the jungle and came hurtling out of the projection. 'Turn it off,' he yelled. 'Turn it off!'

Romana ran to the CET machine and switched it off.

The wall went dark.

The Mandrels were imprisoned in their miniature world once more.

The Doctor collapsed gasping on a couch.

'Well, Doctor,' said Fisk ironically. 'What now?'

The Doctor waved him aside. 'Romana?'

'Yes, Doctor?'

'We've got two minutes and fifty-eight seconds to take this machine apart and rebuild it – starting from now!'

Romana stared at him. 'This machine, Doctor? Tryst's CET machine?'

'That's right.'

'Are you joking?'

'Do I look as if I'm joking?'

Romana sighed. 'I'll need a screwdriver.'

The Doctor produced his sonic screwdriver and handed it to her.

Romana said, 'All right, Doctor. What do you want me to do?'

In the cabin of the *Hecate*, Tryst was adjusting the angle of the encoder laser, attached to his duplicate CET machine.

'How does it look?' asked Dymond.

'Couldn't be better! Are you ready to get us out of here as soon as I've made the transfer?'

Dymond nodded. 'It's all preset. I've switched control through to the computer. All I've got to do is press that button.' He nodded towards the computer console keyboard. 'All right. I'm almost ready ...'

Tryst switched on the CET machine, and rows of lights blinked on its control console.

In the VIP lounge, the Doctor and Romana were working at frantic speed. 'Increase the gain on the matrix modulator,' ordered the Doctor.

Romana adjusted a circuit. 'Up five points.'

The Doctor shook his head. 'It's not enough, we need more power.'

'We could put jump leads on K9,' suggested Romana.

'Good idea! Here, K9, come and put your leads on.'

Obediently K9 glided forward. Romana attached leads from the CET machine to his antennae. 'All connected, K9?'

'Affirmative, Mistress.'

Stott and Costa were looking on in astonishment. 'Doctor, what *are* you trying to achieve?' asked Stott.

'To put it briefly, we're trying to increase the range and power of this rather ramshackle machine. How many points now Romana?'

'Ten and building, with K9's help.'

That's more like it. I think we're going to be all right!'

The Doctor reached inside the machine to make a final adjustment. Suddenly a beam of violet light shot through the hull of the ship and connected with the machine, making it hum with life.

The Doctor gave a yelp of pain and snatched back his hand.

'Doctor, are you all right,' asked Romana.

The Doctor blew on his fingers. 'Just a bit of a shock.'

The eerie violet light played over the machine.

Stott looked at Romana. 'What's happening?'

'It's from the *Hecate* – they're making the transfer,' she whispered.

'That means we've lost, they can get away!'

'Quiet,' snapped the Doctor. 'Romana, reverse the setting on the transmutation matrix!'

Romana hesitated.

'It's all right,' said the Doctor. 'It's quite safe.'

Suddenly the violet beam of the encoder laser cut out.

Romana looked at the Doctor. 'Surely it's too late now. They've already made the transfer.'

'Romana, will you please reverse the setting on the transmutation matrix.'

Muttering to herself, Romana obeyed.

The Doctor turned to K9. 'Track the *Hecate* for me, please. Give me her exact co-ordinates.'

'Affirmative, Master.'

The Doctor leaned over the machine and operated the rejigged controls.

In the cabin of the *Hecate*, Tryst completed a careful check of his duplicate CET machine. 'It's all here, all safely transferred. We've done it, Dymond. Now get us out of here!'

Dymond reached for the computer keyboard and pressed a switch.

The *Hecate*'s engines roared into life.

The survey ship streaked off into the blackness of deep space.

K9 was calling out the *Hecate*'s co-ordinates. '47.3 vector 799 – in seven seconds.'

'47.3 vector 799. You'd better be right, K9.'
You'd better be right, K9.'

The Doctor counted off the last few seconds, then threw the switch.

For a moment the room seemed to blurr and shimmer, then everything returned to normal. 'Good!' said the Doctor happily.

'What happened?' demanded Stott.

The Doctor patted the CET machine. 'Ever heard the expression "hoist with his own petard"? Refers to a kind of early bomb. It was so unreliable it often blew up the man who was using it. Something very similar's happened here.'

Fisk came storming into the room. 'I've just come from the bridge, Doctor. Our instruments show that the *Hecate* is now in deep space, well beyond reach. Whatever your plan was, it has failed miserably. There's absolutely no way we can catch them now!'

14

Electronic Zoo

The Doctor rose, yawned, stretched, and slapped the furious Fisk heartily on the back. 'On the contrary, my dear chap, I've already caught them.' He touched a control on the CET machine and the cabin of the *Hecate* appeared on the wall screen, complete with Dymond and Tryst staring out of the screen in astonishment.

The Doctor waved expansively at the screen. 'There you are – all yours! Trapped in their own electronic zoo.'

'But ... but ... but ...' spluttered Fisk.

'What did you do, Doctor?' asked Stott.

'All I did was increase the range of this machine here. Then I used it to bring them back. Matter transmutation, you see! Since the projection is still unstable, all you have to do is pluck them out!'

Fisk waved to his guards. 'You heard the Doctor. Go and – pluck them out!'

The astonished guards went gingerly into the projection, seized the even more astonished Tryst and Dymond and dragged them out into the lounge. Dymond let himself be marched out in sullen silence, but Tryst dragged his guards to a halt before the Doctor.

'Doctor, please, I never wanted to be involved in all this. Tell them I only did it for the sake of science, for the sake of funding my research. You understand, don't you, Doctor? You're a scientist too ...'

The Doctor gave him a brief glance of utter contempt. 'Go away, Tryst. Just – go away.'

Still protesting, Tryst was dragged out by the guards.

Tryst was the worst kind of criminal of all, reflected the Doctor, the kind who sincerely believes that however appalling his crimes, there is always a perfectly valid excuse.

A short time later, the Doctor, Romana and K9 were saying goodbye to Stott and Della outside the TARDIS.

Relays of shuttlecraft were ferrying indignant passengers down to the delights of Azure, and the Doctor had decided to sneak away before Fisk could involve him in his unending series of enquiries.

'How are you feeling now, Della,' asked the Doctor.

'I'm fine, now that the nightmare is over.'

Stott smiled and put his arm around her protectively.

The Doctor held up a laser crystal. 'The nightmare is safely imprisoned here – in the Eden crystal.'

Romana held up a whole case of crystals. 'And here's the rest of Tryst's electronic zoo.'

Della flushed. 'It was never meant for a zoo. It really was a conservation exercise – for some of us.' She smiled up at Stott.

The Doctor said, 'I think the best way of conserving the poor creatures imprisoned in these crystals would be to project them back to their home planets, don't you?'

Della nodded eagerly. 'Oh yes!' Then her face fell. 'But you've already dismantled the CET machines.'

Romana smiled. 'Don't worry, we've got some very sophisticated projection equipment in the TARDIS.

Do it in no time – literally! '

'What about the Mandrels, Doctor?' asked Stott. 'They *are* the source of the Vraxoin, after all.'

'That isn't their fault, is it? The Mandrels have a perfect right to exist too, on their own planet and in their own way. You must quarantine Eden, Major Stott, make sure no one else discovers the secret.'

Stott nodded grimly. 'Don't worry, Doctor, we'll take care of it. The Mandrels will be able to live in peace for evermore.'

Romana looked down at the rack of crystals. 'You know, I can only think of one animal who'd be happy in an electronic zoo! '

'What's that?' asked Della.

Romana looked down at K9 and smiled. 'I don't think it would be tactful to tell you – do you, K9?'

'Negative, Mistress,' said K9 huffily, and glided into the TARDIS.

The Doctor and Romana said their goodbyes and followed him.

Stott and Della turned and walked off down the corridor. A few seconds later they heard a strange wheezing, groaning sound.

They turned to look, but the corridor was empty. The TARDIS was on its way to new adventures.